BULLWHIP

by
John Dyson

Dales Large Print Books
Long Preston, North Yorkshire,
England.

British Library Cataloguing in Publication Data.

Dyson, John
  Bullwhip.

A catalogue record for this book is
available from the British Library

ISBN 1-85389-619-5 pbk

First published in Great Britain by Robert Hale Ltd., 1994

Published in Large Print March, 1996 by arrangement with
Robert Hale Ltd.

Dales Large Print is an imprint of
Library Magna Books Ltd.
Printed and bound in Great Britain by
T.J. Press (Padstow) Ltd., Cornwall, PL28 8RW.

BULLWHIP

A beautiful Mexican woman is the bait provided by the hated *guardia rural* to tempt Black Pete, outlaw, out of the mountains. Brigand Ramón Corral, now state governor of Sonora, not only lusts after the creole beauty but instigates a 'final solution' of genocide and deportation against the Yaqui Indians. Guns blazing, Black Pete and his amigos go to the young lady's rescue and lead the Yaquis in their fight to hang onto their land.

To Bunty and the bat-eared Jack Russell,
Mole, good friends

ONE

'Kinda sick, ain't it?' Black Pete drawled as he and his companions watched a man being crucified to the oak door of a small mission church.

The man, in the white cotton garments of a peasant, screamed as nails were hammered through his wrists and palms to hold him spreadeagled, face-flattened, upon the door. The *charros* in their tight riding clothes and sombreros laughed to see him hanging there.

Crouched beside Pete in the scrub of trees overlooking the village of Fortuna del Reys, Miguel, a Mexican himself, pushed his leather hat back from his bald copper-bronze dome, and murmured, 'You ain't seen nuthin' yet, *amigo*. This is Me-hico.'

'Can't we *do* something?' Melody pleaded.

5

'It's easy to tell you never lived south of the border, honey,' Nathan Strong, her blond-haired Texan *muchacho*, opined. 'This is how they dispense justice down here.'

The four friends watched as a man dressed in the military uniform of the hated *jefe politico*—political commissar—lounged at a table outside a tavern opposite the church, raised a glass of tequila to his lips and beckoned to a brute holding a coiled bullwhip. 'Lay on hard,' he called. 'Cut deep. These peasants have tough hides.'

Villagers stood at the doorways of their houses. Their dark faces hardly flinched as the lead-tipped rawhide whip sang through the air and cut into the *peon's* back and a first line of blood seeped into the white shirt as if it were blotting paper.

The *jefe* smacked his lips, possibly in appreciation of the tequila, but probably at the finesse of the whip-handler. He crossed his polished boots and lit a cigarette, as if settling in for an afternoon at the theatre. 'Harder!' he cried.

'Who's that blood-thirsty bastard, I

wonder?' Nathan muttered, as the once-white shirt was systematically cut to shreds and stained a sticky mess of crimson.

Short and wiry, he was dressed in the wide batwing chaps and high-crowned Stetson of a cowboy. His vivid blue eyes, usually as peaceful as summer skies, glinted icily cold. 'I say we put a bullet through him.'

Pete scratched at his black beard, thoughtfully. 'Tempting...but I don't think much of our chances, if we do. There's forty armed men down there and we're on their territory.'

A bitter smile twitched his lips as the whip whistled through the air and sliced the *peon's* flesh like a razor. He was taller, and older than Nathan. The tattered macinaw, the narrow shot-gun chaps, and well-worn boots seemed to have moulded to his lean limbs. Beneath his hard-brimmed, low-crowned hat was a mane of smoke-black hair hanging over his collar. 'They have something in common with the Apache, these *mestizos,*' he said. 'They like to see how much

7

a man can suffer. And then some more.'

'*Si,*' Miguel agreed. 'They have the vices of the Spaniards and the Indians without any of their virtues. The great Presidente Diaz is one, himself.'

Both men had assessed from the high-cheekboned, dark hued face of the elegant overseer that he was one, too. And there was sarcasm in Miguel's tone for the only 'great' quality about the president was his cynicism, and the number of rich landowners he had bribed to support his takeover of power.

'Why don't they just hang him and get it over with?' Nathan asked, as he swallowed an uncomfortable lump in his throat. 'These guys are likely to make me bring up my breakfast.'

'Nineteen,' Melody whispered, as she counted the strokes that had flayed the man's back.

The four friends had only recently crossed the invisible, or unmarked, *frontera* from Arizona into Sonora and Melody, for one, was beginning to wish she had

8

not quit the saloon and whorehouse Black Pete had given her to run at Fort Sumner back in northern New Mexico. 'I suggest we hightail it out of here,' she grumbled. 'I don't like the look of these *hombres* at all.'

Pete gave her a faint grin. 'That might be good tactics, *muchacha.*'

'Too late,' Miguel put in, rising to his feet, for one of the *charros* had turned and was pointing up at the hillside at them. His horse had alerted him with a snicker of greeting to their own mounts.

Pete took the reins of his black stallion and led him down through the rocks to the adobe houses, ambling with his long-legged easy gait in order to show that they implied no threat to the company. The *charros* were already turning, with sharp cries, aiming rifles and revolvers in their direction. He strolled on across the dusty plaza towards the scene of the activity. The whip ceased singing as the Mexican *vaqueros* turned to regard him with fierce resentment. His throat felt a trifle prickly, as did the hair at the nape of his head, but he forced himself to go forward. In a situation like this the only weapon for a man was bluff.

'Howdy,' he said, as he paused in front of the elegant military man, and tipped a gloved finger to his hat. 'Having a little trouble with the natives here?'

The *charros'*—or cowboys'—smiles widened at this diversion and one of them screamed, 'Haiyech! *Gringos.*'

The *jefe's* thin lips twisted into a smile as he surveyed the tall *Yanqui* and his companions. They had appeared out of nowhere. 'To whom do I have the honour?' he asked, in a mocking way.

'Pete Bowen. Hope we ain' interruptin' your fun.'

'No, no, not at all. Ferdinand Veraco, Colonel. Take a chair. You are welcome to watch the show, *señor.*'

Veraco doffed his hand in a theatrical manner, snapped his fingers for more tequila and the owner of the *cantina* came running with a jug to obsequiously pour them drinks all round. Well, leaseholder, to be more correct, Pete thought. Few peons owned anything. Most had been swindled out of what little land they had been granted by the Spaniards. This man would probably have to pay back most of what small profit he made to whoever presided over this vast *hacienda* on which he had the misfortune to live.

Colonel Ferdinand Veraco, in his cream uniform with scarlet epaulets, glanced disdainfully at Pete's followers, the fair-cropped cowboy, the Mexican in his rough purple-striped serape, and what he took to be a Mexican boy. He noted their Colt .45 revolvers strapped to bullet-laden belts, and that he was unfamiliar with their faces.

He called to the man with the whip. 'Hey, El Barracho! Why have you ceased? Did I instruct you to? These gentlemen want to see some blood flow. Lay on harder. We haven't heard him scream enough yet.'

Again the whip slashed into the lacerated crimson of the man's back and they were now so close they could see his cruelly nailed palms strain and twitch. The peon

11

gave only a croaking gasp. He seemed to be past screaming.

'Happy days,' Black Pete said, as he took a lick of salt, a squeeze of lemon and raised the tequila. 'Here's to our first visit to Mexico.'

'Not the first,' Miguel corrected. 'Remember, we crossed the border from your ranch at Sombrero Rock to fight the Comancheros.'

'Ah,' Colonel Veraco remarked. 'So you are a rancher.'

'Used to be,' Black Pete gritted out, for he did not like being reminded of those days. 'Long time ago.'

'And what is your profession now?' The colonel's smile was like an insult. 'What brings you to our land?'

'Tourist,' Pete grinned. 'Thought we'd take a look-see, maybe do a little silver prospecting.'

'Really?' Veraco mused, as he watched the whip do its work. 'Harder, El Barracho! Have you no energy? Or would you like a taste of it yourself?'

The great brute of a whip-lasher flung

himself more vigorously into his efforts, as Nathan blurted out, 'Don't you reckon he's had enough?'

'Your young friend is squeamish. There is no such thing as enough for a peon,' Veraco snapped out. 'They should be whipped every day. They are as stubborn as mules. Lay it on, I say.'

'Thirty,' Melody silently counted, only her lips moving.

'It's on account of his age,' Pete mused, hoping Nathan didn't do anything foolish. What could they do surrounded by forty men armed to the teeth who enjoyed such sport? 'Us Texans are a mite sentimental. We don't like to kill folk, less we really need to. What exactly has this fellow done, if you don't mind me enquiring?'

'Done? He has had the temerity to refuse a favour to his master. Don Ignatio Lazar. General Lazar. Perhaps you have heard of him? He owns this land for two hundred miles in every direction.'

'Cain't say I have,' Pete remarked, fiddling with the makings of a cigarette in a corn husk, Mexican-style, putting it to his lips and striking a match on his boot. 'What favour was that, Colonel?'

'Would you believe?' Veraco smiled. 'This peon has actually managed to produce two very attractive daughters. Did you not know, Don Ignatio has seigneurial rights over all virgins?'

'Nope,' Pete said, pursing his lips as he sampled another glass of the powerful liquor. 'Didn't know you still practised that sort of thing.'

'Indeed, my master had the first girl when she was fifteen. He quickly tired of her. She works in our kitchens now. Would you believe, this moron has refused to hand over the second girl? He says he has sent her to your country for safety. It is a lie. He has hidden her somewhere.'

The bullwhip cracked like a pistol shot in the air and flashed out across the peon's buttocks, cutting his baggy trousers away, making the *charros* laugh.

Several more strokes followed, striping the white skin of the buttocks and blood trickled down the man's thighs.

14

'OK, that is enough,' Veraco called. 'Will he talk now?'

One of the *charros* grabbed the peon by his hair and spoke violently to him, but turned and shook his head, glumly.

'Right. Let him hang there all night. He should be ready to talk by sun-up. If not, he gets more. There is always a breaking point.'

'If death doesn't get him first,' Pete put in.

'No, we will keep him alive, Just,' Veraco laughed. 'We are experts.'

'Where do you think she is?' Pete asked in Spanish, by way of being conversational.

'Ach! Who knows? These peasants have all kinds of little hidey-holes in the hills. They try to cheat Don Ignatio of goods and pesos that rightfully belong to him.

'Don Ignatio has been too liberal with them. Don't worry, my friend. She won't get away. We will find her. If her father doesn't talk we will shoot every peon in the village one by one until somebody does.'

'How long has Don Ignatio been their

master?' Pete asked, blowing out smoke in the colonel's direction, his eyes narrowed. 'No doubt he benefited from Diaz seizing power?'

'Indeed, that is so. This hacienda was given to him. Porfirio Diaz believes in being grateful to his supporters. He gives millions of pesos to those who might be of use to him, to establish his liberal democracy.'

'Democracy?' Nathan scoffed. 'Dictatorship we Texans call it.'

The colonel eyed him as if amused by his naïvety and went on, 'The president believes in the policy of *pan ó palo*. Bread or the club. He has offered gifts and privileges to all those who might oppose him, the army, the clergy, the landowners, even the chiefs of the bandit gangs who ravened this land before him. If they accept they are his friends. If they don't, he kills them. The result is, my friend, for the first time we have peace in Mexico. The first time since independence so many years ago.'

'Very neat,' Pete mused. 'Instead of the

wolves fighting each other they now join forces in attacking the sheepfolds.'

'Exactly.' Veraco smiled his brittle smile and pushed across a tray of lemon sprinkled *jicamas*. 'For a *Yanqui* you are very perceptive.'

'I ain't a Yankee. I rode for the Rebels.'

'Ah, one of the noble Confederates! What rank did you achieve?'

'Loo-tenant. Thirty-second Texan Volunteers. But'—he shrugged and took a bite of *jicama*, passing the fly-buzzing tray to his friends—'that, too, was a long time ago.'

'I am interested. These men you see before you, what do you think they are?'

'They look like pig-shit cowboys to me,' Nathan grinned, reaching for the tequila bottle.

Only a slight flinch to the flattened planes of Veraco's face indicated he had heard the remark. 'They are the scum of the prisons, murderers, thieves, rapists. All hand-picked by me. Their only qualifications are that they can ride and kill. In return they have sworn allegiance to me

17

and to Don Ignatio. I call them my Wild Dogs.'

El Barracho—the Drunkard—staggered over, his great belly stretching out a filthy shirt, sweat oozing from the pores of his puffy face, and placed his fists on the table. 'Can I give him some more, *jefe?*'

'Oh, very well.' Veraco recoiled from his sweaty stench, placing a perfumed handkerchief to his nostrils. He pushed over a bottle of tequila. 'Here! You have done well. Open the flesh. Let me see the white of bone.'

El Barracho took a pull from the bottle and lurched happily back to his task. As the whip snaked and cracked Melody turned her face away as if she might gag. Mentally she continued to count the strokes.

'He may be a pig but he has great finesse with the whip, wouldn't you agree?' the colonel smiled.

'Maybe,' Pete muttered. 'So these ain't *charros?* They're your private army?'

'Not exactly. I am paid by the government to raise a militia. We have to be on

18

the alert for infiltrators, subversives. You would be surprised how many people try to stir up trouble. We have to make sure that the population thinks correctly, that they appreciate all that the great father, Porfirio Diaz, is doing for them in far off Mexico City.'

'You mean you kill anyone who dreams of freedom,' Nathan said.

'Your young friend is rather irritating, is he not?'

'It's only his way,' Pete said, tensing as the whip spat. 'You get used to him.'

'I am the leader of the pack. You see how grateful El Barracho is to me—for his freedom, for the horses and guns I provide him, for his bottles of tequila. If I gave the word he would tear you to pieces.'

'He could try. Didn't I hear you say this Don Ignatio was your master, Colonel? How come, if you work for the government?'

'Do you suppose a gentleman such as I could live on one salary?' The colonel winked and raised his glass. 'No, I also use my *charros* as Don Ignatio's private army. He has forty other *vaqueros* to herd his cows for him. The trouble is my men do not have—how do you say?—a lot of milk in their coconuts. We have a war on our hands with the Yaqui Indians. My *charros* do not have much idea of military tactics. You men, you look as if you know how to use those guns.'

Black Pete grinned and, as if by some sleight of hand, one of his .44s was slid from beneath his macinaw and the nozzle stuck up the colonel's nose. Veraco's smile froze. Pete squeezed the trigger and a shot crashed out, startling humans and horses. The peon screamed as the nail in his hand was thudded harder into the door by the impact of the bullet.

Veraco's face relaxed. The bullet had almost taken his ear off. He glanced, nervously, at the peon. 'Well, at least, you made him scream, my friend, which was more than we could do.'

'That nail weren't knocked in deep enough.' Pete broke the frame of the revolver, spun the cylinder, inserted another bullet.

The Mexicans had become a bristling hostile ring, revolvers and rifles covering the *gringos*. With a flutter of his fingers Veraco indicated to his men to put their guns away. 'A nice piece you have there.'

'Yep. It's the latest model by the three Wesson brothers and their new partner, Mistuh Smith. Double action, self-cocking, no need to use your thumb, centre fire. Guess you're still using rimfire down here. Three safety catches. A range of two hundred and fifty yards. Beauty is I can use the same .44-calibre bullets for my Winchester. Don't have to carry two kinds. Your own hardware looks a bit antiquated, if you don't mind me saying. This revolver is perfection of the art. I don't see how it can be bettered. I wouldn't mind betting this design will still be in use in a hundred years time.'[1]

---

[1] Pete's prophecy was correct. A century later the US police use them.

'Impressive,' the colonel remarked. 'But you still have to know how to shoot. Are your comrades as adept?'

'Taught Nathan myself. The boy there's still larnin'. Toss a handful of them empty bottles up.'

As the *charros* did so Miguel's twelve inch long barrel appeared from his cross holster, and Nathan's old Navy Colt was lifted high—KAROOM! Each of the two dozen bottles burst in mid-air amid wild whoops of admiration.

'Señor Bowen'—Varraco leaned forward and offered his hand—'I think General Don Ignatio is going to be very interested in meeting you. I am going to recommend that you join our private army as adviser.'

Black Pete made a wry face and scratched his beard. 'Don't rightly remember sayin' we was for sale.'

'You won't find a better silver mine than the general,' Veraco said, looking around at the grinning *charros*. 'And I hardly think you have any choice. *Pan ó palo*, remember?'

Melody was only glad that the gunplay

had made the grunting El Barracho cease his ministrations to the back of the peon nailed to the church door. She had counted to fifty.

TWO

The four friends, surrounded by the Wild Dogs on their spirited mustangs, approached what appeared to be a fortified monastery, its walls six feet thick and its battlements thirty feet high. To one side, dwarfed by it, were the bamboo and wattle huts of peons who serviced its fields and its kitchens.

'Behold,' Veraco cried. 'The home of my master.'

Nobody could fight the Church, as yet, in this land. The Church was vastly rich and had the people's minds. The crafty Diaz had recognized this and had returned many of the confiscated church properties, making them his grateful allies. Indeed, the building had once housed brothers, but they had been turned out by the former 'progressive' regime.[1] It had lasted no longer than most. He had hung on to some, however, and given this one to Don Ignatio.

They had crossed the green Sonoran plain to reach this region of strangely shaped hills and, as they galloped through the high wooden gates, the look-out ringing his bell, the elegant Veraco shouted, 'We have company. The governor is here.'

This was apparent from the lavishly dressed men of the Guardia Rural in their huge sombreros, and silver-embroidered suits of grey suede, who milled about the monastery's grand courtyard. They carried red blankets over one shoulder, crimson badges of authority to spill blood. Their

---

[1] A pure-bred Indian, Benito Juarez, presided over a constitution that confiscated church property, abolished special privileges for the military, divided land among the poor, and called for freedom of the Press, free hospitals and schools. He died in office in 1872. Diaz subsequently established a totalitarian state with himself at the head of the pyramid.

saddle horns, bridles and spurs flashed with silver.

Veraco greeted several of them, stepped down and gave his reins to a peasant who ran forward.

'I will inform Don Ignatio and the governor we have *gringos* as guests,' he smiled. 'They might care to receive you.'

'That guy's smile sure gives me the heebie-jeebies,' Nathan drawled, when he had gone. 'What you doin', Pete? You tryin' to box us into a corner?'

'*Si,* I thought this trip to my country was going to be holiday,' Melody agreed. 'It is rapidly turning into nightmare. That poor man. Can we not do something for him? Why you shoot at him that way? Wasn't he suffering enough?'

Pete shrugged. 'I ain't happy about that li'l guy any more than you,' he gritted out.

But his mind was distracted by a peon who was trying to catch at the bridle of his prancing black stallion. 'Stand back, man. Jesus don't take kindly to strangers touching him. And all these li'l filly

26

mustangs around is gittin' him heated up. Jest lead the way.'

The ostler wisely did so, padding forward on huraches[1] to the extensive stables, blacksmith's shop, and corrals at the far end of the great courtyard. While his friend's mustangs were put into the communal corral, the peon realized that this fiery horse needed to be kept apart. They clopped past a long line of shady stalls until they found an empty one.

'Be good to him,' Pete said, and flipped the ostler a quarter. 'We come a long way. He's got a son or daughter back in Injin Territory I want him to meet one day.'

He glanced in at the next stall and whistled with awe. A magnificent white beast was stomping about in there, his neck proudly arched, his nostrils widening as he gave a regal whinny of indignation at the presence of another stallion so close by. He had the arched nose and power of the pure-bred Spaniard, but something also of

---

[1] Cheap, rope-soled, cloth shoes.

27

the graceful Arab in him. A horse among horses.

Pete put out a hand to him.

'Be careful, *señor*. He has killed two grooms. His kick is like lightning.'

'A savage devil, eh? Now why would that be?'

'You see the blood stain in his eye? A sign of viciousness. We call him Excellency. He is the horse of Don Ignatio. The finest horse in his herd. Only the head *charro* can handle him.'

'You don't say? Too slim in the leg for my liking. Built for the flats, not mountain work. Fast, eh?'

'The fastest, *señor*. His excellency's pride and joy.'

'Even more than his virgin brides?'

'I do not understand, *señor*.'

'Very diplomatic of you to say so. You don't like the whip? Neither, I guess, does that horse.'

'What you say about the whip?' Melody asked, as they arrived from the corrals. 'What got into you Pete? First you shoot that poor man, then you show off with your guns. This not like you.'

Pete put a cheroot into his mouth and gave a clenched-teeth grin as he looked around. 'I reckoned we had to show them Wild Dogs some fancy shootin' before they put us to the test, themselves.'

'I get your meaning, *amigo*,' Miguel said. 'But, with all these *rurales* around, how we goin' to get out of here?'

'We will bide our time,' Pete said. 'I figure, instead of going looking for any silver mine, there might be plenty of silver for the taking about here.'

'You goin' to be hired gun for these devils?' Melody exploded.

'Mebbe so, for a while.'

'Keep cool, honey,' Nathan said. 'And keep that durn poncho on. We don't want any of 'em suspectin' you're a gal. You might find yourself in Don Ignatio's private bordello.'

'Yeah, that occurred to me.' Pete eyed Melody, who had her long black hair tied up under a wide sombrero, a shawl half-masking her face and wound around her slim throat, and a heavy poncho

29

camouflaging the fulsome curves of her young body, her legs swathed in tasselled leather and boots. Strung with bandoleers of bullets, a carbine across her back, and revolver in her belt, she passed, at first sight, for some wild-looking *bandido*. But, what if they had to sleep in a communal room with the other men?

'I've heard about this Sonoran governor, Ramón Corral. More blood-thirsty than any bandit. He's a legalized assassin,' Pete muttered.

'Maybe we should do Mexico a favour and assassinate *him*,' Melody suggested.

'If you are keen on meeting your Maker in a very painful manner,' Pete replied. 'Me, I reckon on a few more years to enjoy this sweet life. Talking about that, let's take a look at the cookhouse. Ain't that an aroma of chilli beans drifting across?'

His keen nostrils led the way to the kitchens where several cooks were making ado preparing food over red-roaring stone ovens. They were presided over by a large be-smocked lady, dark of complexion, eyes and hair, who greeted them with a scowl. Miguel gave her protuberant buttocks beneath her skirts a fierce squeeze, grinning evilly at her, and growling in his throaty voice, 'I'd like to take a dip into your melting pot, *señorita.*'

'Some *señorita!*' Nathan said.

The cook smacked Miguel on his sun-blackened bald dome with her ladle, screaming at him to begone but, as he wound an arm around her double-barrelled waist, she gave a flicker of a smile beneath a pencil-thin moustache, elbowing him away, but in a half-hearted manner. She parrot-squawked some words to one of her minions who began to double-bank four plates with a rich tomato sauce and pinto beans.

'What a terror he is,' Pete chuckled. 'Straight in there for the growl and grunt.'

'Growl and—?' Melody echoed. 'What is this?'

'Oh, an English lord I once worked for as a hunting guide came out with it. He said it's Cockney rhyming slang. Kinda like...er...making love.'

'And from what I heard,' Nathan put

in, 'you were pretty soon growling and grunting with that milord's wife.'

'Waal, that was her idea. She had a voracious appetite.'

'That's what I got, an appetite,' Melody said, and grabbed a plate of beans, and began spooning them up.

'You keep clear of these two *hombres*, honey,' Nathan grinned. 'They both a coupla meat-mongers. I'm surprised they ain't tried to steal you away from me.'

'Hey, we're *amigos*,' Pete said sharply, as he, too, began to dig in. 'Not that I would be averse to dipping into her dilberry bush, if she was free. Man couldn't help notice she had a mighty cute figure that time she took a dip in the Gila.'

'You keep your eyes elsewhere, you randy ole bastard,' Nathan growled. 'Or one day you and me might be testing our shootin' skills.'

'Taught the boy all he knows and that's the gratitude,' Pete said, but, in fact, his eye had begun to wander over the other female cooks and scullery maids for it had been a long ride across the deserts and some while since he had had a woman. He generally preferred someone with a little more pedigree, but such waterholes were few and far between.

It had been a long time since his wife had been killed and he and his son had been driven off his Texas ranch. Pete had executed the cattle baron responsible and sent his son to live with an aunt in Kansas. Since then he had ridden as an outlaw. Often he had a hankering to settle down again with a decent woman, but whenever he met a suitable candidate trouble seemed to step in the way. Yes, it had been a long while he had been riding. It had become a way of life now. He had thought maybe they would leave him in peace if he came south of the border. But, there sure didn't appear to be much peace to be had in these parts.

THREE

The *gringos* were summoned to a great banqueting hall, with a high vaulted ceiling, furnished with religious oils of angels in the clouds and carved statuettes of pious saints (what could they think of the treacheries plotted in this place?). Being mere Mexicans, Melody and Miguel were not invited. The ageing Don Ignatio was slumped in a high carved oak chair, his withered limbs clothed in a cream uniform of similar style to Veraco's, but with more medallions, ribbons and scarlet braid indicating his general's rank. His sallow face was flecked with 'coffin spots', his thin grey hair slicked back, and his eyes glassily bloodshot as they glimmered from puffy pouches. 'The *Americanos*,' he said, indicating with a shaking hand that they come forward and be seated.

'Howdy,' Pete replied, touching his hat, politely.

He wondered how a fifteen-year-old girl would feel to be subjected to the embraces of a man like that. Not very enthusiastically, he presumed. A man who had the power of life or death over all his peons.

'We left him hanging there,' Colonel Veraco was saying. 'I am certain by the morning he will be ready to talk.'

'As long as you do not kill him,' the old man said. 'I would not want you to do that. I like my girls to be grateful to me.'

Another man was sitting beside Don Ignatio. He was in the uniform of a *rurale*, but with much more fine silver embroidery and ornate silver star medals pinned to his jacket. His tightly clothed legs were stretched out, propped on the cruel rowels of silver spurs. His well-fed belly was covered with a scarlet sash and a white ruffled shirt was open at his thick throat. His face was dark and coarse, a luxuriant moustache, as was the fashion, hanging about his jowls. He had the arrogant cruel air inherited by so many from their Spanish forebears. Ramón Corral, Pete assumed.

'I would not waste a bullet on such curs,' he snapped out. 'There's plenty of rope. Hang them one by one. How dare they defy you, Don Ignatio? Make them talk.'

'No, gentlemen,' Don Ignatio quavered. 'I try to treat my people like a father his children. I am sure this man will see sense.'

The humgumptious old devil, Pete thought. Does he really believe he has the right...?

The watery eyes focused on him, assessing him, and Don Ignatio said, 'I understand you witnessed a little scene this afternoon. Unfortunate, but necessary. I wouldn't like you to get the impression—'

'Cut the humbug and get to the point,' Nathan said.

The governor let out a roar of laughter. 'Ah, the straight-shooting, straight-talking Texan!'

'That's the way we are,' Nathan said.

'Maybe you are drifters. Gunslingers. The scum of the frontier,' Colonel Veraco replied, with his icy smile. 'Your government might thank us for returning your heads. They might even pay us bounty.'

'They ain' got nuthin' on me. I'm a former federal investigator and sheriff. Washington would confirm that. If you laid a finger on us it sure wouldn't look good, wouldn't improve international relations. Pete here was a renowned US deputy marshal and respected rancher and trail boss. 'Fore things went wrong.'

''Fore things went wrong,' Veraco repeated. 'What are you now? Outlaws on the dodge? Nobody would give a damn if we shot you out of hand.'

'Gentlemen,' Don Ignatio protested. 'Let us not have ill-feeling. The president himself has instructed us to welcome *Americanos*. We want their trade. We want them to invest in our poor country. Why, a foreigner is as important as a general or a bullfighter in Mexico.'

'So?' Pete asked, helping himself to a

37

Havana cigar from a box on the table. 'Why you wanna see us?'

'To welcome you!' the governor shouted. 'One *bandido* recognizes another, eh?'

'The governor has a sense of humour,' the head of this vast hacienda cackled, revealing some glistening gold teeth among the rotten stumps. 'He can afford to. How much did I hear they were paying you, Ramón, two hundred thousand monthly in pesos out of War Department expenses? On top of your double salary as civil and military chief?'

'I have the upkeep of my lifestyle to pay for,' Corral grinned through his whiskers. 'Though, I admit, Don Porfirio has indeed been benevolent towards me.'

'I ain't particularly keen on bein' your hired gun if all we do is go around torturin' and hangin' peasants,' Nathan drawled, tossing off his Stetson and rubbing fingers through his golden crop.'

'No, let me explain,' the old man said. 'We would not request you to perform any tasks like that, necessary sometimes as they may be. No, we are having trouble with the

Yaqui Indians. They occupy the borders of my territory, fertile Sonoran land to the east. I have tried to reason with them but their chief, Cajeme, has declared war on us. I want you to protect my people against the depredations of these savages.'

'We done some Indian fightin' in our time,' Nathan replied, scratching at his crotch. 'Man has to on the frontier. That don't sound too bad. But we were planning on heading south further into Chihuahua, investin' in a silver mine.'

'Such investments are greatly welcomed by President Diaz, but not always successful,' Colonel Veraco said. 'From what I gather of your past you two men know how to handle weapons. We would not be ungrateful.'

'Name your price, gentlemen,' Don Ignatio offered. 'We may be able to come to terms.'

'How about five hundred dollars a month in advance, all found, extra horses, ammunition and guns provided if necessary, and a free rein to smoke these Indians out for you?' Pete suggested, pursing his lips, gazing at the ceiling as he blew a smoke ring.

'You price yourselves high,' the governor remarked.

'Not as high as you, Ramón,' Pete smiled. 'The same for our *compadres.*'

'Ach, no, not Mexicans. They come ten for a cent,' the colonel snapped.

'Not these boys,' Nathan drawled.

'OK, let us be agreed,' the old man interrupted. 'Five hundred dollars a month for you two. One hundred for your Mexicans.'

'Sounds reasonable, don't it, Pete?' Nathan asked.

'We could give it a try,' Pete replied, taking off his own hat now that business was concluded. 'All this palavering sure gives a man a thirst.'

'Bring the aguardiente,' Don Ignatio called. 'And the key to my safe.'

'Glad to have you ride with us, *gringos,*' Corral shouted across the table, with his roar of laughter. 'Maybe we teach you a thing or two.'

'Maybe,' Pete sighed, as he reached a

long arm out for the bottle of brandy and filled a glass to the brim. 'Or maybe we teach you.'

He raised the glass to his lips, tipped it back, and muttered, 'Salud!' as its heat coursed through his veins.

FOUR

The blare of the *rurales'* bugles, the thudding of an Indian drum, the clash of cymbals, and the fast thrumming of guitars filled the great banqueting hall with a cacophony that stirred the blood and set boot heels tapping.

'Viva! Vaya! Ole' the governor of Sonora roared as a haughty gypsy woman, her shiny black tresses drawn severely back, flashed the scarlet silk flounces of her underskirts, and arms hovering, castanets chattering, soared like a ship in sail as her partner, in formal Andalusian black, stomped and strutted about her.

Pete and Nathan had been invited to feast on mutton and corn and to watch the assembled entertainment. Their heads were beginning to spin from the firewater as they watched a bevy of young women spin and swirl, barefooted, their shapely bronzed thighs revealed as their peasant skirts billowed. They had been rounded up to supplement the celebrated visiting dancers. The old raper of virgins, Don Ignatio, licked his lips lasciviously, as he watched them.

When they were at last allowed to rest, breathless and sweat-streamed, serving women, in low-cut bodices, moved among the *rurale* officers and bigwigs carrying trays of delicacies or leather skins of red wine. They were stocky, thick-waisted peasant women with broad faces. It is unlikely any of *them* were virgins. Ramón Corral snatched a wine skin from one and squeezed a jet of the crimson liquid into his open mouth. The woman squealed like a parrot as he pulled her on to his knee. There was a hysterical feel to her forced gaiety.

'Hey, *gringos,*' Corral called over to them. 'You wan' woman you have one. You have as many as you wan'. Tomorrow we head for the mountains.'

Black Pete stumbled to his feet, possibly over-emphasizing his drunkenness. Nathan caught him before he fell flat upon the loaded tables and grinned. 'We ain' had no sleep for two days. Time to turn in.'

'Pah! *Yanquis!* What are you, monks like Veraco here?' the governor shouted—he seemed unable to speak without a bull-roar to his voice.

Colonel Veraco watched Nathan hoist Pete over his shoulder and lumber towards the door. He raised one eyebrow, suspiciously, as he sat composed and neat as ever in his cream uniform. He ignored the governor's remark. He was not one to dally with common women.

'I ain't averse to payin' for it,' Pete said as Nathan hauled him down the corridor. 'But when it comes to forcing some poor *pablona*[1] at the point of a revolver I git a kinda bad taste in my throat.'

There was a maze of corridors in the ancient monastery, numerous chambers

---

[1] pablona: working woman.

and carved balconies. It was, in fact, like a small, compact, feudal village, with its own church, shops, bakery, great yards and outbuildings. It even had a swimming pool dug into the rock at the back of the banqueting hall, surrounded by patios and fountains, the height of luxury in such an arid region.

'Jest what I need to sober me up,' Pete said, as they emerged beside it, and he leaped fully-clothed into its depths, whooping and swishing back his long hair as he splashed about. He looked up at the starlit sky and the battlements, listened to the thump of drums and blare of bugles. His head was still reeling but he had a plan in mind. 'You think anyone would miss me if I took a night ride?'

They found the room they had been allotted. Miguel was growling and grunting beneath a bundle of blankets with the fat lady cook. And Nathan rolled in beside Melody while Pete tipped water from his boots. He stripped off, found a dry black wool shirt in his pack, borrowed Nathan's jeans, which were a trifle short, thonged his gunbelt tight, clamped his hat back on his wet hair and hissed, 'See you in the morning, *amigos*. I don't fancy listening to your amorous murmurings all night.'

He took his lariat, returned to the patio, and sent his rope snaking up to an overhanging buttress. He hauled himself up hand over hand, straddled the top of the wall, jerked the lariat up, and tossed it to dangle down outside. He glanced around but there were no sentries about. He lowered himself to scramble down safely outside the monastery walls. He had landed almost in the backyard of one of the bamboo huts scattered about. And, just what he needed, there was a mule hobbled, which gave a bray of indignation at being disturbed.

'Quiet,' he whispered to it as the occupant of the hut, a peon in white pyjamas, poked out of his door to see what was going on. He had a machete in his hand. Pete prodded a Smith and Wesson into his back. 'Hold it, *muchacho*. I'm gonna hire this mule for the night. You know nothing, understand?' He pressed a handful of silver pesos into the peasant's hand. 'You breathe a word I come back and put a bullet in your brain, savvy?'

'*Si, señor.*' The peasant found him a rope bridle and crude wooden saddle, and some sacking to muffle the mule's hooves.

'Reminds me of that durn ornery critter I had in Abilene,' Pete muttered as he dragged the recalcitrant mule out into the road, struggled aboard, and loped off into the night.

FIVE

'*Señor*, be merciful. Kill me now. I cannot stand the pain any more. Don't let me sacrifice my daughter. She is so fine a girl. Tomorrow when they come I must surely talk.'

The cruelly whipped man was sagged in the chill moonlight against the church door, suspended by the nails in his smashed and lacerated hands. 'Throttle me,' he begged. 'Make it appear as if my heart has stopped.' His torn shirt was stiff with blood.

The aguardiente Black Pete forced into his parched lips brought him some life back. 'Why haven't the villagers set you free.'

'They would all be killed if they so much as tried. No, don't release me, *señor.*' His dark face beneath a shock of grey hair twisted away from the door so he could squint at this *gringo*. 'What do you want with me?'

'I want to help you,' Pete whispered, insistently in fluent Spanish. 'Where is your daughter? Tell me where I can find her so I can take her somewhere else, some cave in the mountain. So, even if you do break, you won't be able to betray her.'

'How do I know this isn't a trick? That fiend Veraco has put you up to it, hasn't he?' A cold sweat had broken out on the man's forehead from the effects of the alcohol and he spoke with effort, huskily. 'Why should I give you my daughter? She is too good for the lecher.'

'You sure got some gizzard, ole feller,' Pete muttered. 'Any other man would probably be dead by now. But, you can't last for ever. You gotta believe me. I wanna help that gal.'

'Why? So you can have her yourself and throw her on the garbage pile afterwards?'

'C'm on! You think I like riding this rickety ole mule miles through the moonlight? Risking a bullet when I could be safely tucked up in bed? Maybe I'm crazy, but I'm her only chance. You know that. Maybe I fancy putting Veraco's nose out of joint. Spit it out. I ain't got much time.'

The man stared through solemn haggard eyes at him. 'My daughter is no ordinary girl, mister. She is a Creole, part aristocrat Spaniard. Her mother was a daughter of the then *haciendado*. A woman with noble blood in her.'

'How come?'

'I was not always old and bowed. I was strong and lusty when I was young. I worked in her stables as head groom. We men are not the only ones with appetites. She wanted me, that high-class lady. Unbelievable as it may seem. These things happen.'

'You mean, she had a child by you?'

'*Si, señor.* Secretly she was born, at the convent. To avoid the shame. At her request the nuns gave the baby girl to me and my wife to raise.'

'You don't say,' Pete breathed. 'Come, let me release you. I will get you both back

50

to the good old US of A. Why worry about these cowards?'

The crucified man closed his eyes and gasped with pain. 'They are my people, mister. Do not make them suffer. Leave me. I trust you. You will find her in the cellar of the old windmill.'

'What is your name, old feller?'

'Manuel Varga. My daughter is Louisa. Do what you can for her. Go with God.'

'And you, Manuel. You are a fine man. A good father. I'll leave you now.'

Veraco was so sure that nobody would dare help old Varga that he had left no sentry on guard. Louisa! Pete thought. Strange! It had been his wife's name.

Black Pete had noticed the dilapidated windmill that had fallen into disuse back along the rockstrewn trail. He climbed through a dusty hole in its side and probed around, striking a match, by which light he saw a pile of planks which appeared to have been too carefully placed. He pulled them aside and found a cellar flap. He jerked it up and called into the dark hole,

'I am a friend. You can come out. Your father sent me.'

Whoever was down there hesitated. But, if he were friend or foe there was no way she could resist. A wan face appeared, dark eyes peering through a tangle of black curls. Pete offered his hand and pulled her out. He struck another match and saw a girl of about sixteen with a well-formed body apparent beneath her patched shawl and skirt. Her face was delicately carved, and there was fire in her eyes as she stared at him.

'Your ole man certainly wasn't kiddin',' Pete said, with awe. 'No wonder Don Ignatio is hungry to get his hands on you.'

'The pig. I hate him,' the girl hissed. 'Where is my father? What is happening?'

'He's been...detained. He won't take my help. His last wish is that I get you to safety. But, where? Have you any friends? Are there any caves around here where you could hide out for a while?'

'There is no such thing as safety in

Sonora. The *rurales* will hunt me down. Everybody is terrified of Veraco and the governor. Maybe it is best I stay here?'

'Nope, you cain't stay here. Come on, Louisa. Jump up behind me on this mule. Maybe you'd be safest in the wolf's lair.'

There was a glimmer of dawn on the eastern horizon as Pete re-hobbled the mule, gave its anxious master more pesos, found his rope and climbed thirty feet up the monastery wall. He peered over the top. There were only a few *rurales* squatted around a fire in the courtyard. He signalled to the girl and she hoisted herself up agilely enough. They quickly regained the interior of the courtyard.

Pete removed his boots to lead her silently through the stone passages lit by oil flares. Suddenly he heard the sound of gruff voices, the clinking of spurs and heavy bootfalls approaching. He froze. There was no place to hide!

He gave a rebel whoop which echoed along the corridor. 'You the cutest little chickadee I ever did see. Ahm gonna take you home to Tennessee,' he sang out. 'Yes, siree!'

Louisa backed away, startled, as he grabbed hold of her. The bootfalls were getting nearer. Soon they would appear around the corner. Pete squeezed fingers about her firm breasts—he'd got to give a realistic impression!—flattened her against the wall and stooped to seek her lips with his own, covering her face with his head. 'C'm on, *muchacha*. Less do it 'gain.'

The men ceased talking. Their clatter of spurs drew alongside. Pete felt Louisa's hand snake up to fondle the hair at his nape and one of her bare legs wound around him. He grimaced to one side as he kissed and groped at her and met the eyes of two *rurales*. All they could see were two heads of dark hair intertwining. Pete winked at them.

One gave a snort of laughter. 'The *gringo's* still drunk.' And they ambled clattering on.

Louisa's lips were moist and open to his. Slowly she let her bare knee slide down from his thigh, and her hands pressed him away.

'Hang on,' he murmured, a tremor of desire going through him for the girl.

She pushed him off, haughtily. 'Stop it!' she hissed.

'Guess I got carried away,' he said, a twinkle in his dark eyes. 'And you young enough to be my daughter!'

He noticed a narrow spiralling staircase to one side. 'Better try up here. Maybe it leads to one of them balconies or belfries.'

They climbed high up into the old building. When he saw a wooden door he pushed it open. It appeared to be a disused store. There was a straw palliasse among the cobwebs.

'Here,' he said, 'make yourself at home. I'll try to get some food and water to you. You're gonna have to bide here a while, Louisa. Let's hope it's the last place Veraco will think of looking.'

Her skin was a pale *café-au-lait* colour. Not dark like the *mestizos*. Such a girl was much valued in Mexico. Her cheeks had flushed peach,—what with?—indignation, or kindled passion? Her hazel eyes flickered with fire as she stood before him, as if defying him—or wanting him—to touch her again. He reached out and pressed her hands with his own and had the satisfaction of feeling them tighten in response.

'Don't worry. We'll get you out of here.'

But, as he hurried back down the spiralling stone steps he thought, I must be goin' loco. They'll probably slaughter us all.

SIX

Feared as they might be, the sight of a hundred Mexican horsemen sweeping out of the great monastery gates hung low over the necks of their wild-eyed mustangs, their spurs and bridles jingling, galloping by with wild cries in their cloud of dust...such a sight could bring a sense of awe to the soul of even the most downtrodden peasant.

Some forty *vaqueros* were led by Colonel Veraco on his long-striding chestnut, its pale mane and tail flowing, impeccably harnessed, its hide glowing. The Governor of Sonora, Ramón Corral, charged proudly at the head of his platoon of *rurales* in their scarlet and grey uniforms and wide sombreros. Black Pete and his three *amigos* were somewhere in the middle of them all.

Old Don Ignatio had been left to sport in his swimming bath tended by three half-naked *hacienda* women. The bath had to be cleaned and refilled frequently from the village's scarce supply. His was the height of decadent luxury in a thirsty land.

They rode at a steady lope through the day and by nightfall, when they made camp, the *barrancas* and *cañons* of the distant mountain ranges had appeared starkly out of the heat haze.

A tent, collapsible chairs and table, had been carried on a separate horse and this was set up for the governor to lord it before the campfire, his great sombrero, heavy with silver conchos, tilted across his eyes, and his glistening spurs stuck out.

Beside him sat Colonel Veraco, clean shaven, his boots polished, fresh from his *toilette*. Their men sprawled around their various fires amid the drifting smoke and scent of *frijoles* cooking.

Ramón had a carofon of Cuban rum and it was quickly making him garrulous. 'You are as cold as a reptile, Veraco, you know that? I don' like you. I don' like you at all.

Me, I kill and torture a man because I have to, but you, you enjoy it, don't you?'

Ferdinand Veraco made a down-turn grimace of his thin lips and sipped at his glass of rum. The governor bellowed with laughter and reached over to slap his knee.

'I don' like you. Tha's why I made you *jefe politico* for this area. You hear that? So you can kill and torture legally. I want these Yaquis subdued and you are the man to do it.'

'Who will their lands go to?'

'Aha! Who do you think? Some to me. Some to Diaz, and, as you sweep the Indians away some of their lands can be added to Don Ignatio's hacienda. Or maybe a hacienda of your own?'

The colonel's eyes glimmered, greedily. 'What kind of profit would these lands bring?'

'Beyond your wildest dreams. No doubt you know that Don Ignatio pays less tax on his estates than a street pedlar? So also will you. You must be grateful to me, Colonel.'

'I am, indeed. It is an honour, Governor.'

'Be sure you serve me well. One day I may wield even more power than that of State governor. I may yet be president, myself. You hear that, Black Pete? Come over here and drink with us.'

Pete got up from his nearby fire and ambled over, a tin mug of coffee in one hand. 'Howdy, gents. Heard you say somethun about gittin' as rich as Croesus. Such talk always makes my ears prick up.'

'Sure,'—Ramón Corral tipped rum from the gallon jug into the mug—'you serve me well and you, too, may benefit. Why, we might even find you a small estate to ranch. Or maybe the rights to a silver mine. Loyalty is rewarded in this land. There are plums for the picking and we distribute them to the deserving ones.'

'By deserving I take it you mean those who prove themselves the most murderous bastards in your bunch?'

'Hi-yech! These straight from the hip Texans. You've got it. In a nutshell.'

'Waal, Governor, I always try to earn my

pay.' Pete sprawled in a vacant chair and lit a cheroot. 'That sounds an interesting offer.'

He listened to one of the *rurales* strumming his guitar and said, offhandedly, 'By the way, *jefe,* how did you get on with that dumb-head you flogged yesterday?'

'Ach!'—The colonel disdainfully flicked the ash from his cigarette. 'We gave him another session this morning. He talked, but he either lied or the girl had fled. She won't get far. I am afraid El Barracho laid on too hard. Manuel Varga died shortly after they took him down.'

'Too bad,' Pete shrugged.

'So the general don' get his virgin?' the governor grinned.

'He will get her. I am pursuing my enquiries. I pity anyone who raises a hand to help her.'

'What's she like?'

'A beauty. The pale skin of a Creole. There is a rumour that she has noble blood.'

'Pure Spanish thoroughbred, eh? Get her, Veraco. Get her for me, not the general. With a wife like that a man could really rise to the top of the pile in Mexico.'

Pete reached for the *carofon,* slinging the jug on to his shoulder, tipping the rum to his lips. He looked out at the jagged black claws of the mountains silhouetted against the purple night sky. 'How much further to the Indian lands?'

'Another day's ride to their main village,' Veraco said. 'By the way, Texan, what happened to your finger?'

Pete looked at the stub of the middle digit of his right hand. 'A bullet. Some durn bounty hunter. It was the last thing he did.'

SEVEN

When they reached the valley of the Yaqui River the horsemen followed its course until they saw the mission church cross above the Indian village of Honi. They charged at speed through its bamboo brakes giving wild blood-curdling cries, revolvers at the ready.

A deputation of elders, their harsh faces impassive, waited to greet them as they rode into the dusty plaza. The houses were square block hogans in the middle of fertile fields, irrigated by narrow man-made canals where corn, squash, melons and peaches grew.

'Where is Cajeme?' the governor shouted at them, not deigning to descend from his horse. 'I, the Governor, have come all this way to parley with your chief.'

An ancient warrior, a beaded headband holding his long grey hair close about his dark wrinkled face, stood resolutely before the mounted gunmen, and gave a vague wave of his hand. 'He is in the mountains.'

'The right place for him. He can skulk up there like a wolf,' Ramón Corral shouted. 'Let it be known, once and for all, that you have no right to these lands.'

'These lands are ours.' The old man's voice trembled with rage as he stood before a group of about fifty elders, women and children. 'The Spanish *conquistadores* gave them to us for ever. For hundreds of years and many more before that, since the beginning of time, they have been our lands.'

Like the rest of the villagers the old man was dressed partly as a *vaquero*, leather leggings and an embroidered velvet shirt, and partly Indian, a half-skirt and moccasins, beads and wampum coiled about his neck. He carried an ancient long-barrelled musket which might, from its enscrolled silverwork, have belonged to a *conquistadore*. He dug into his shirt pocket and produced a yellowed piece of parchment. 'This was given to us by the Spaniards and later agreed by the great *presidente,* Santa Ana.'

'General Santa Ana ain't president no more,' the governor growled. 'You have a new president now and he says you must give up this land.'

'Never,' the old man hollered, brandishing the rifle. 'Cajeme would never agree to that.'

Ferdinand Veraco leaned from his horse to snatch the parchment. He sat and studied it. 'This is completely out of date. Have you not heard of the law passed in 1856? All common lands, under that, were seized and divided in fee simple among the peasants. Don Ignatio Lazar has purchased these rights and is the new owner.'

'Yes,' the governor snarled, reaching for the parchment and contemptuously tearing it to pieces. 'You have been warned to get off these lands. Why are you still here?'

'These are our lands,' another of the elders cried, stepping forward, raising his

65

machete, threateningly.

The governor pulled his revolver and shot him point-blank in the chest. The old man tumbled back, blood flowing, as the black powder cloud swirled. For seconds the villagers were poised in a frieze of horror and then they began to howl and clamour in protest.

It was the signal for the *rurales* and Wild Dogs to charge into them slashing at the villagers with sabres, brandishing guns, galloping after any who tried to escape, lassoing them and dragging them back to the plaza with wild shrieks as if they were rounding up a herd of cattle.

'What are we going to do?' Melody cried, as they whirled their own horses amid the clouds of dust and screaming children.

Black Pete saw El Barracho lop a running toddler's head from his shoulders as if it was no more than a coconut. Instead of milk spurting, there was blood. The mother was down on her knees screaming. The Drunkard reached down and dragged her away by her hair.

'Hell knows!' Pete gritted out, drawing one of his Smith and Wessons'. What could they do against a band of more than ninety trained killers?

None of the villagers escaped. They were jostled into a ploughed field behind the small mission church where they were disarmed. Most were too old and frail, or too young to put up much of a struggle against the heavily armed horsemen.

'What shall we do with them?' Veraco asked.

Governor Corral gave his barrel-chested laugh and stroked his moustachios. 'I have been offered thirty-five dollars a head for them if they are delivered to the mines at Yucatán in irons. But—who needs money?—what would you do, *jefe?*'

'We need to set an example. Show Cajeme what will happen to the Yaquis if he dares to defy us.'

'What do you suggest, hang them?'

'No.' Veraco snapped out orders to his men. 'Bury every one up to their necks in this field.'

'Yeehaii!' Corral whooped, cracking his

bullwhip to snake around the neck of the old Indian who had acted as spokesman, dragging him off his feet. 'This one dared to defy me. Me, the Governor! I want him to be buried first.'

Pete, Melody, Miguel and Nathan watched tense-faced as the horsemen found spades, dug deep holes, and thrust the struggling and protesting Indians into them.

'What about the children, *commandante?*' one called.

'Yes, women, children, babes in arms. All of them I said,' Colonel Veraco shouted in his shrill voice as he strutted about on his fine chestnut horse supervising the proceedings.

It took time, but eventually all that could be seen on the ploughed field was a crop of dark Indian heads, sullen and helpless, dotted about the red earth. Only the babies and small children cried. The others, women and men, stayed silent, somehow proud.

A trickle of sweat ran down Black Pete's temple, and a chill up his spine, as he sat his stallion in the baking sun, torn between a fierce urge to start shooting at the *rurales*—damn the odds!—and a dull realization of his powerlessness. He watched a table and chairs set up and Ramón Corral and Veraco served a bottle of *tequila*. Something nasty was about to happen and Pete had a pretty good idea what.

The *rurales* and Wild Dogs were milling their horses impatiently at one end of the field.

'Charge!' Veraco shouted, brandishing his sabre.

The mass of cavalry thundered away down the field, and whoops of excitement mingled with the screams of their victims as steel shod hooves kicked up clods of bloody flesh, bone, brains and hair. They galloped back and forth trampling the remains of the Yaquis into the red earth.

EIGHT

They moved out the next morning—leaving Honi a village of vultures and ghosts—and followed a tributary of the Rio Yaqui. On their flank was the great citadel of the Sierra Madre, the centrepiece of the mountain spine that runs from Alaska to Cape Horn. Somewhere up there were eyes watching the line of horsemen as they climbed through the great rocks bordering the snaking stream.

The air became clear and sharp as they rapidly ascended the steep trail until they were many thousands of feet above sea level. Soon cactus and mescal gave way to piñon. The Yaqui village of Metallos was perched on an outcrop of rock above a ravine. As they entered its square it was strangely silent. As before only a small

70

defiant band of elderly and infirm faced them. The warriors, with some of their women and families, had fled.

'Round them up,' Ramón Corral yelled. 'We will march them back to Guaymas. We might as well make some money from them. This is where I leave you.'

The Mexicans crashed their horses into the wooden houses dragging out any Indians who had tried to hide. Any who tried to escape were summarily shot under the law of *ley fuga,* the law of flight. To try to evade 'justice' in Diaz's Mexico was a capital offence.

'Not much of a haul,' the governor said, glumly, as he sat his horse and surveyed the fifty or so sullen prisoners, elders and children, roped together by their necks. 'Not to worry, my friend, we will round up more as we return. I will leave you twenty of my *rurales,* Veraco. Any Yaquis who make war on us must be killed. I will offer a reward of seven dollars for every pair of Yaqui ears. Soon these people will be no more.'

He raised his hand, a *rurale* gave a jerk on the rope, and he led the column out of

71

the village. 'You know what do, Veraco,' he shouted back. 'Put them to the flames. Kill any who resist.'

The mute Indians were dragged after the horsemen. They faced many hundreds of miles of hot, punishing marching until they reached Guaymas, a port of the Pacific coast. From there they would be shipped south to San Blas. They then would have to undergo a fifteen day march across the mountains to San Marcos and on by rail and boat to the tropical jungles of Yucatán in the far south. Only about a third of all the prisoners deported would survive.

Veraco's force headed on up into the mountains leaving the smoke of burning villages to mark their trail.

'How much longer are we going to hang about with these butchers?' Nathan asked, as the four friends sat around their separate campfire one night.

'*Vamones o otro lugar*—let's go somewhere else,' Melody pleaded.

'What about Lousia? We gonna jest leave her for Don Ignatio?' Pete frowned and lit a cheroot from a glowing twig. 'I don't like

72

this no more than you do. You all know if we try to take on these boys we will be shot down like dogs.'

'Ramón controls the whole State,' Miguel agreed, as he cleaned his Colt Peacemaker —known as a Buntline Special—with its extra long twelve-inch barrel. He fitted its detachable carbine breech to it and squinted along the sights. The new weapon saved him the necessity of carrying a heavy rifle. 'He's got this State stitched up tight as a rug. If you want out we could make our way over the State line through the mountains to Casas Grandes, Chihuahua. Or you got some other plan, *amigo?*'

'I'm working on it,' Pete muttered. 'We came here to get rich, didn't we?'

'Not by spilling innocent blood,' Nathan said. 'That ain't my style. And I didn't think it was yours, Mistuh Bowen.'

Pete, for once in his life, had no caustic reply to give. He bowed his head, staring into the embers. 'I'm turning in. We have some hard riding tomorrow.'

'Some hard killing, too, no doubt,' Melody said when he had gone.

73

NINE

'I haven't seen you *gringos* showing much enthusiasm for this operation. You are supposed to be Indian fighters. How do you suggest we mop up Cajeme's men?'

Ferdinand Veraco was having breakfast in his tent at the break of dawn as his men saddled their mounts. He had summoned Pete before him. His cream uniform was looking worse for wear, blood-spotted and dirt stained, but he was clean-shaven and alert, his boots polished by one of his men to a shine. He eyed the black-bearded Texan coldly, 'Well?'

'If you ask me you're going about this the wrong way. We ain't got the best reputation in America for Indian-dealing, but in Arizona General Crook had the right policy. He offered the Apache land,

74

showed them it would pay to live peaceful. He enlisted a good company of Apache scouts to lead them to the hostiles' lairs. You ain't gonna enlist any Yaqui scouts. You're killin' 'em all.'

'Pah! Your great General Crook was removed from his post for being too soft. It took a hard man, Miles, to finally burn them out. That's what we will do here.'

'Waal,' Pete drawled. 'Maybe. But the Yaquis know these mountains like the back of their hand. I cain't see Cajeme surrendering. Not after your massacres and deportations. From what I hear he ain't the sort to lay down and be kicked. These Yaquis are fierce warriors. Even the Spaniards knew it was wise to leave them be.'

'This is defeatist talk,' Veraco said. 'Why, we have offered them land but they refused to move to it.'

'Huh!' Black Pete spat a gob of brown baccy juice that landed on Veraco's shiny boot. 'A small piece of waterless desert, that's what you offered them.'

'You foul desert rat!' Veraco used a

cloth to wipe his boot clean. 'They are only savages, man. I want them killed. How do we go about it? That's what I'm asking you.'

'Waal, I'd say we head into that section of mountains there where we've seen the mirrors flashing from. Spread out your forces, make a wide sweep of two pincer movements. Keep to a pre-arranged timetable, agree a system of communication. Six rapid shots indicates trouble. With any luck we might flush 'em out.'

'Hmm.' Veraco, who had little experience of mountain fighting—he was more of a political man—mused over the advice. He had no great liking for the collection of former *bandidos* he rode with, nor did he trust the *gringos*. What was he doing in these hills? There was a silent sinister quality to the dark *barrancas* that rose before them. Could Cajeme be up there somewhere? There was only one way to find out. 'It sounds a reasonable plan.'

'Sure beats leading a column straight into one of them cañons. That way you're asking to be wiped out.'

'Right.' Veraco got to his feet. 'You take the right flank. I'll take the left with my *vaqueros*. The *rurales* can go through the centre. *Andale, gringo.*

'Get going, yourself,' Pete said.

Ten of the Wild Dogs were deputed to ride with the *gringos* led by the swaggering, brutish El Barracho, who was always the first to volunteer his services if a prisoner required flogging or torturing.

'I guess Veraco don't trust us on our own,' Pete said. 'These boys keepin' an eye on us.'

He had stepped down from his mount to study a path that branched off from the rushing stream. 'Tracks of a mule,' he muttered. 'Made recent. And a man. Wearin' *huaraches* or sandals. Maybe he's lookin' for Cajeme, too? Fill your canteens. Water's gonna be our big problem in these hills. We'll follow him.'

Darkness came early, shadow running over them as the sun bled away on the high peaks. 'Keep the fire low and your

77

voices down,' Pete instructed. 'There's gonna be a full moon. Nice night for an Indian attack, if they're anything like our Apache friends.'

El Barracho, however, scorned such precautions, or, perhaps, was too drunk to take care. He had a large goatskin of aguardiente to keep himself topped up, swilling it furtively, unwilling to share it with the others. Soon he was staggering around the fire, tripping over canteen and firewood, cursing and shouting.

'For Christ's sake,' Nathan growled. 'We might as well tell the whole damn Yaqui nation where we are. We're in enemy territory now you knucklehead.'

'Hai! *Gringo!*' El Barracho sprawled beside him, grinning his unshaven jaws. 'What's the matter? You scared of a little Yaqui man?'

'You're pretty brave,' Nathan said, pushing off his embrace, 'when it comes to killin' wimmin and kids.'

The Drunkard cackled with laughter and turned to Melody. 'Hey, who is this pretty boy? You stay close to him, huh?

What is he, your *amor?* You one of those *homosexuales,* Texan boy?'

He began stroking Melody's cheek, teasingly. She had already been finding it difficult to disguise herself, keeping her heavy poncho on to hide her curves in the midday heat, having to seek out somewhere secluded for her toilet. When the Wild Dogs urinated carelessly in front of her she pretended not to notice, or be concerned by their lurid oaths, their cruel, crude behaviour, The former bandits had no pretensions to be other than brutes.

'Hey, I ain't so sure he is a boy,' El Barracho cooed. 'His skin's as soft and sweet as a little *muchacha.'*

'Keep your hands offen the kid,' Nathan said bristling, getting to his feet. 'Jest shut your mouth you greasy stinkin' pig.'

'Hai! There's one test to find out.' The Drunkard's great paw dived down to grope into Melody's loins. She squealed, trying to wriggle out of his grasp.

Nathan caught him by the back of the collar, hauled him around, and cracked him a punch to the side of his jaw. El

Barracho flicked his head as if he had been irritated by a fly.

'Pig, is it?' The bandit slid out his long hunting knife and clambered to his feet, towering over Nathan, almost twice his weight and size. 'Come on, *gringo*, I'm goin' to cut your little blond scalp off. You know what they call me? El Gorgo—the Big Man.'

'The Big Mouth,' Nathan said, standing his ground. 'C'mon, fatso.'

'Hech!' El Barracho grinned, gappily. 'And when I've eaten you for supper, you know what I'm gonna do? I'm gonna have the little *muchacha*. Because that's what I think he is, a girl. And, if he isn't? So! I ain't bothered either way.'

The knife flashed in the firelight, slitting the shirt above Nathan's waist, and a sliver of blood appeared. The Drunkard was faster then he appeared to be. Nathan backed to one side. He had earlier unhooked his gunbelt and laid it aside. He was unarmed. El Barracho gripped the knife tight and made another slash. Nathan seized his massive forearm as it passed and swung his boot up to thud into the big man's groin. El Barracho groaned and went cross-eyed. But he stayed on his feet and forced a grin, the knife still in his hand.

'Unk!' he said, as Miguel's twelve inch barrel revolver buffaloed him on the back of his thick neck. This time he slumped to his knees and collapsed in the ashes.

Miguel spun around, covering the *vaqueros* with the big Colt. 'Let him sleep it off,' he said. 'Maybe we should hogtie him, too, to keep him out of trouble. Then douse this fire. Me and Pete will take first watch.'

Pete crawled on his belly through the rocks, his knife in his hand, hoping he didn't put his elbows on any wandering tarantulas, scorpions or eight-inch centipedes, the bite of which could play havoc with a man's nerves. As if they didn't have enough trouble with Yaquis! He had manoeuvred out from the camp, moving in a circle so that he might cut across the approach of any Indian.

The moon had risen high, a great

silver sterile ball illuminating the rocks a ghostly grey. He listened, intently. A sinister hooting sequence, a code of four, penetrated the night. He had heard the call before: the spotted screech owl, a native of Mexico, which also haunted the big canyons of Arizona. Or was it?

He lay alert as the night wore on. To his ears came a more plaintive hooting, softer, nearby. He rolled over to look behind him. Only the dark silhouette of rocks. That would probably be the tiny insect-eating elf owl. No doubt had a nest in one of the stunted oaks that grew in the gullies. Or was it? He put his hand to his mouth to make the soft answering call. There was a rustle in the undergrowth nearby and something leapt out. Pete's muscles tensed. He relaxed as he saw a small big-eared kit fox step into the moonlight.

There was another rustle behind him. He rolled back over to avoid, just in time, a lance, its iron tip scraping off the rock beside him. As the Yaqui hurled himself upon him he swung his knife up and penetrated his abdomen, twisting the blade hard. The Indian gasped and slumped heavily upon him.

Pete felt warm blood seep over his hand. He pushed the lithe young warrior off and stabbed him again to make sure.

He looked up and saw another Yaqui crouched on a boulder above him, a bow pulled taut, poised to aim. A shot crashed out and the Indian gave a frenzied leap as his spine was blasted apart. Miguel ran forward, his smoking Buntline Special in his hands. He knelt on the crest and fired again, the shot whining and ricocheting through the pass.

'He got away,' Miguel grunted, as Pete joined him.

The third Yaqui had disappeared into the maze of rocks. 'Reckon they were a scouting party. Otherwise they would all be on us by now.'

The Wild Dogs had run from the camp to see what was going on. 'Ain't no use going after them in the dark. Nathan and a couple of you boys better take next watch. I'm gonna git me some sleep.'

He looked down at one of the Wild

Dogs who was busy slicing off the Indians' ears.

'What'n hell you doin' now?'

'You heard Ramón.' The man waved his bloody trophy. 'These are worth seven dollars a pair.'

'Hell,' Pete said. 'You guys!'

TEN

'Sure could do with a mug of tea,' Pete muttered, as he stirred at the thick black coffee in the pot.

'You an' your tea,' Melody smiled.

'Got the taste for it when I worked for that milord an' Lady Lucy. Perfumed stuff all the way from China it was, though I prefer plain Injin. Find it settles the stomach better than coffee.'

'You got a bad stomach, Pete?'

'Yeah,' he grinned, ruefully. 'Guess it's a touch of Montezuma's revenge. Must be bad water. Or them red hot chillis. Playing havoc with my gut.'

'Or the firewater! Don't you worry, Pete. I'll boil you up a nice potion of mountain herbs.'

'Yeah, that might really finish me off.'

'If Cajeme don' get to us first. You think he's aroun' here, Pete?'

'Wouldn't be surprised if his band ain't holed up in some cave. I'm sorry to have got you into this mess, Melody. It's all kinda got outa hand.'

'Yes.' She went to look down at the bodies of the Indians, the early morning flies already buzzing about their bloody earless heads, the ants starting on their eyes. 'Why do people have to be so cruel? They are only youths. They are only defending their own.'

'I reckon it's them or us out here.'

'Can't we bury them?'

'Nope. No time. I'll put them up on them rocks. The eagles and foxes will soon tidy them up.'

'Eugh!' she cried, crossing herself.

'C'mon, honey,' Nathan drawled. 'You gotta act like a *bandido* or El Barracho will be pawin' you some more.'

'Eugh!' she spat out again.

The Drunkard had a stupid, puzzled look on his face as his comrades untied him. 'What happened?' He rubbed the

86

back of his neck. 'Who hit me?'

'You get a bullet,' Melody shouted, 'next time you touch me.'

'Hey!' He grinned widely. 'I remember. The little *muchacha*. Tonight, I get yoo-ou!'

'Douse that fire,' Pete said. 'We're riding out.'

At noon they came face to face with a man and a mule. He was middle-aged, his dark hair greying, garbed in a hair smock and sandals. He was kneeling, taking a frugal meal of *tortilla* and water. His burro was nibbling at some oak-leaved branches. And by his side was a little dog, a bat-eared terrier, who was lapping at a bowl of water.

'Hai-yaaiieee!' El Barracho yelled. 'What have we here?'

'Breaking off them branches sure made it easy to follow you,' Pete said. 'What you doin' here, mistuh?'

'I seek a way over the mountains. A way out of this province. It is a province of death.'

87

'Hai-yech! It sure is,' El Barracho said, giving his horse a rest from his great weight, stepping down, bandoleers of bullets draped about his barrel chest. He took the man by his hair, slammed him up against an oak, put a knife to his throat and growled, 'What are you? A priest?' The little dog started barking furiously and jumped up to bite at his buttocks. 'Leave us be,' the man said. 'I am Brother Francisco. I ran the mission at Honi. Before you massacred all my people.'

'Mission!' El Barracho jeered into his face kicking the terrier away. 'They don't need missionaries. These people are savages. Heathens. They don't believe in Christ.'

'Nonetheless they are a good people. They had a good way of life. At least they had before you murderers came. Don't you hurt my dog, you fiend!'

'Murderers! You call us murderers?' El Barracho thudded the brother's head back against the tree. 'We are the law. You are the traitor. *Comprende?*'

'Maybe he knows the way to Cajeme's

hide-out?' one of the other Wild Dogs said. 'Maybe he was going to warn him.'

'If he does he will soon show us the way.' El Barracho thudded the priest's head back and forth, grinning as he did so. 'Won't you, Francisco?'

As he paused, Francisco spat in his face. 'I will tell you nothing,' he shouted. 'You deserve to rot in hell. All of you.'

At this the angry dog renewed his attack on the big *vaquero's* ankle. Barracho stepped back, shaking the terrier off, wiping the spittle from his face, looking childishly hurt. 'You see what he did? Him, a priest? You hear what he say? Hand me that bullwhip. Tie him to that tree. We will soon see if he change his mind.' The terrier stared, dismayed.

The *vaqueros* took hold of the priest, laughed as they ripped his smock apart to reveal his bare pale back, and began to rope him to the oak.

Nathan slowly, and slyly, pulled out his old Navy Colt, a pre-Civil War weapon converted by the Richards system in 1871 from loose powder and ball to rear-loading metallic cartridges. It had a standard eight-inch barrel. He thumbed the hammer and squeezed the trigger. An empty chamber clicked. He kept one like that for safety while he was in the saddle. He thumbed the hammer again, his blue eyes staring, maniacally, as he waved it at the Wild Dogs. 'Now jest you hold on,' he drawled.

'Ha! Li'l blondie!' El Barracho grinned, as he turned. 'What you wan', *mi corazon?*'

'Jest you leave him alone. I've had enough of this.'

'Ah, we play too rough for you? Why don' you go home?'

'Jest leave him, thassall.'

Black Pete stepped down from his horse and stretched, casually, pulling the macinaw back from his gun butts. 'What's the trouble?' he said. He stooped down to pat the terrier, pushing him aside. Miguel and Melody also discreetly moved away from the firing line.

'This li'l *gringo* asshole ain' givin' me no orders. What you think, you can fight all of us?'

'I can try, pigface. I got five li'l leaden

friends in here and the first one's gonna be for you, 'less you step aside.'

'I step aside for no one,' El Barracho shouted, pulling his gun-butt down, blazing away from the holster.

A dozen or more hands flashed to grab at the guns in their belts. The Wild Dogs were backing away, wildly crashing out shots, spinning and tumbling as they did so. Nathan stood firm, his first bullet ricocheting off El Barracho's gunbelt, his second piercing his great gut, knocking him backwards. He fanned his hammer along the line of men.

But, three were already dead, shot through the heart and head by Pete's twin Smith and Wessons as he fired double-handed. Miguel's Buntline long-barrel double-action, held in both of his hands, accounted for three more. While Melody produced a sawn-off carbine from beneath her poncho and, her face grim, sent one of the detested *vaqueros* spinning into oblivion.

The horses shrilled and kicked, pawing the air with fear as the explosions echoed along the cañon. As the smoke cleared they saw that two of the Wild Dogs were injured, one trying to crawl away on a shattered knee, screaming in agony. Miguel put a Manstopper in his back. The other whimpered as he clutched his bloody arm. *'Adios!'* Nathan whispered, as he stepped over, blew his brains out.

'Watch out!' the priest shouted.

El Barracho was sitting tumbled below the oak tree, blood spilling from his gut into his hand. But his right hand still gripped his revolver in its holster which he was trying to aim at Nathan.

Pete raised his heavy .44. A crash blasted out. A neat red hole appeared in El Barracho's forehead. His head jerked back, his eyes staring.

'He ain't gonna bother anybody again,' he drawled.

El Barracho slumped into death. His intestines exploded with a loud windy trumpeting. Miguel's white teeth flashed in his dark face as they all began laughing. 'That asshole sure knows how to blow his last fanfare!'

Even the priest had to smile his relief 'I expect even Saint Peter heard him. He will be closing the gates quickly.'

The terrier jumped up into his arms, his tail wagging frantically, licking his master's face.

ELEVEN

'Aincha gonna say prayers over 'em?'

Nathan was reloading his old Colt with its filed-down hammer. The slightest touch to the trigger—it was like a hairspring. He had taken it apart, washed, oiled and cleaned it so often it was like his own hand, a part of him.

'Their souls can rot forever in Purgatory for all I care.'

'You're a funny kinda priest, aincha?'

'I am not a true priest. I am a brother. A brother of the revolution from now on.'

'You lost your faith?'

'I have lost my faith in the New Testament. There comes a time when one cannot forever turn the other cheek. I have lost my faith in the Church. I believe in the God of the Old Testament. The God of Vengeance.'

'An eye for an eye?'

'Who said prayers for the Yaquis?'

'Come on,' Pete said. 'Let's get away from these stinkin' corpses. The buzzards can have 'em.'

Miguel was going through their pockets and saddle-bags collecting what silver pesos and valuables they had. 'We should take the guns and ammunition belts. And the horses. Maybe, if we get in a fix, we can trade.'

'Yeah. Bundle 'em up. Bring 'em along.' He eyed Brother Francisco. 'You know where Cajeme is, doncha?'

'The big man's whip would not have got that information out of me.'

'Yeah, well, why ja think we took these bastards apart? I seen plenty of mindless killin' in my time, but what's been goin' on here is a little too one-sided for my liking.'

'Are you saying you want to help the Yaquis?'

'Not in the long term. We're not about

95

to get into a full-scale war with the Mexican Government. No way. But,' Pete pondered, 'maybe we could give 'em a temporary hand. You see, there's somebody I got to go back for.'

'You are a hired gun, a killer. What would you get out of this?'

'Maybe, sometimes, I jest do things for my own satisfaction. A few scores to settle. And, who knows, there might be something in it for me.'

'You crafty old polecat!' Nathan yelled. 'What plot you hatchin'?'

'Not sure,' Pete said, swinging into his saddle. 'See how it goes. How about you, Francisco?'

'I will take you to Cajeme. You have a straight way of talking. I cannot guarantee he will not kill you.'

They did not have to go far across the desolate peaks, however, before they saw they were surrounded. Alerted by the shooting Cajeme had come to look for them. 'Uh-uh!' Nathan muttered as he saw the Indians rise from peaks and boulders all about them, arrows fixed, lances poised. If it had not been for the presence of Brother Francisco they would probably all have been slaughterd on the spot.

Francisco called out to the Indians in their own language and eventually, warily, the Yaqui warriors climbed down from the rocks to close in on them. One of them was taller, more broad-chested and fearless than the others, an obvious leader. His legs were encased in soft leather beneath his short loincloth, his bare arms dark and muscled. He gestured angrily towards them with his spear and Pete could catch a few words of Athapaskan, the language they had in common with the Apache, brought in their journey from the far north. The two tribes had much similarity. Pete gestured at the guns and horses and said in that language 'A gift for you.'

'They are killers,' Cajeme said to Francisco. 'We have watched these men burning our villages, massacring our women and children. Why should we not kill them?'

'They have had a change of heart,' the

brother replied. 'Accept their help. Today may be our day of revenge.'

Cajeme appeared puzzled. His features were dark as carved mahogany, his jutting nose aquiline beneath his hood of shiny crow-black hair. Into a thong fillet were inserted two eagle feathers, and pendants hung from his ears. His sleeveless poncho was of brightly-woven geometrical design and hung down around his hips. Beneath it showed the haft of a hatchet. He had a short bow on one arm and a quiver of arrows on his back.

'This is a trick,' he said. But he was obviously keen to examine the armaments that Miguel had unrolled from their blanket. 'We could easily take these guns from you.'

'You don't have much time,' Miguel told him in Spanish, brandishing an arm at a *cañon* on the other side of the crest. 'There's thirty *rurales* over there. And not so far off another thirty *vaqueros*, Colonel Veraco's killers. They will have heard the shooting.'

'Why you kill those men?'

98

'Because we wanted to. We want to help you, *comprende?*'

Cajeme nodded, solemnly. He indicated to his warriors to help themselves to the guns. Some, although they were not used to such creatures, jumped on to the mustangs, and rode wildly away. Cajeme, Pete, his three friends, and Brother Francisco, followed more soberly, the rest of the band of about fifty Yaquis leaping on foot along the rocks as agile as deer.

'Haiyaii!' Miguel yelled, his savage Spanish voice echoing across the *cañons* as he sat his restless mustang and waved his Buntline Special at the dustcloud of oncoming *rurales* on the valley floor. 'This way.'

Black Pete, on his black stallion, who pranced and pawed the air, showed himself on the skyline, beckoning them with his rifle to follow. He indicated a path up through the narrow sandy-bottomed defile of the arroyo by which they could reach the ridge. And disappeared from sight over the crest.

The *rurales* ploughed onwards, single file, their mustangs slowed by the sand and the steep gradient, unaware that they were riding into a trap. Nathan had already taken up his position, squinting through the telescope sight of his ancient M1847 rifle, a six-shot .44. The telescope ran the length of the long barrel. It was one of Sam Colt's early experiments that had not caught on. He could have taken out the leading rider but he waited for them to draw near, to get within arrow shot. All around him concealed in the rocks Yaquis were squatted their bows drawn, or the Wild Dogs' guns in their hands, peering keenly through the rocks like birds of prey about to pounce. It seemed strange to Nathan to be fighting on the Indian side. But it felt good.

Pete and Miguel had left their horses with a Yaqui boy in charge of the others. They slithered back to the ridge and peered over, Pete pulling his fifteen-shot Winchester into his shoulder. Closer and closer the *rurales* came until they could hear the creak of their harness, the deep breathing of their horses, the muttered curses of the men.

Tzit! An arrow sped silently, pierced the throat of the leading rider. He gurgled and slowly toppled backwards off his mount. Tzit! Tzit! Tzit! More arrows rained down.

'Ambush!' one of the *rurales* cried, struggling to turn his floundering mount. A bugler began to sound the retreat until he, too, was cut down.

'Fire!' Pete shouted, and a fusillade of lead decimated the *rurales*.

With wild impetuosity Miguel jumped to his feet and began spraying the hated *rurales* with his Buntline. Howls of anger and fear came from the Mexicans as on their swirling horses they tried returning the fire. Lead whined and ricocheted. One hit Miguel's head knocking him backwards. He screamed, clutched his face, and lay still.

The Yaquis were not used to guns. Their bullets went wild, bringing several horses down. The animals screamed and writhed in agony as their masters ran for cover in the rocks. It was no use. There was nowhere to hide. They were brave enough men, but this surprise rain of fire was impossible to fight. Some of them threw down their revolvers, raised their arms to surrender. They gibbered with terror as the Yaquis leaped down the rocks. There were howls of triumph, as they slit the Mexicans' throats, crunched machetes into their skulls. They gave them as much mercy as had been given the people of Honi.

Soon the distraight cries were ended. Soon all the *rurales* in their fine uniforms were dead, bloody and mutilated, lying in grotesque postures about the valley floor. The Yaquis stripped them of valuables. Or mutilated them as a final insult. Pete strode about and put the wounded horses out of their agony. His shots barelled off the cañon walls, but soon there was little to be heard but the whine of the wind.

TWELVE

What could be going on? Colonel Ferdinand Veraco wondered. A second great outburst of shooting echoing through the hills had made him turn his thirty *charros* back towards their right pincer movement. 'Perhaps,' he cried, 'your brothers have found some game to pot.'

It was hard going and some time before they reached the entrance to the narrow sandy-bottomed arroyo from where the shooting had come. A trail of shod hoofprints showed that the *rurales* had gone up there. He recalled the *gringo's* words about ambush and halted his men. The strangely silent arroyo gave him a chill feeling. Veraco had a strong sense of self-preservation.

'We must reach the high ground,' he

said, 'climb up along the ridge of the *barranca*. There seems to be some kind of goat path.'

His thoroughbred chestnut was not used to mountain work, unlike the sturdy mustangs, slipping, protesting, cutting his fine hocks on the rocks. Finally they made the ridge, and Veraco peered down through his field-glasses to the bottom of the arroyo. What he saw made him recoil with shock. Instead of Indian bodies there were the raw and bloody bodies of the *rurales* and their horses.

Colonel Veraco was wearing a fine French kepi-style cap, its peak much decorated. Suddenly, it was torn from his head as a bullet whistled through the air and the crack of a rifle reverberated through the *cañon*. '*Nombre Dios!*' he cried, leaping down from his horse, dragging it into cover.

'That shot came from a mile away,' one of the Wild Dogs muttered. 'That was no Indian shooting.'

'The *gringos!* They have betrayed us.'

'Why?' the *charro* asked, puzzled. 'What

could an Indian give them?'

It was, indeed, a mystery, Colonel Veraco's Wild Dogs were provided with fine clothes, four mustangs, guns and ammunition, a bed, roast kid three times a week, as much *pulque* beer as they could drink, and aguardiente on feast days. They could lord it over the peon population. Corral's *rurales* fared even better. Why should any man want to give that up? It was better than rotting in jail. Surely the *gringo* gunmen had been paid good money?

Veraco was rattled. He had retrieved his kepi, half-shattered by the bullet. This was not to his liking. 'Who are our best marksmen?' he asked.

Twenty of the Wild Dogs foolishly volunteered, before realizing what would be required of them.

'Right! I want you men to make your way along the mountainside. Flush out these *gringos*. Bring me their heads, you hear?'

The chosen *charros* took their rifles, but scowled a trifle reluctantly up at him as he climbed on to his horse. They looked along at the vultures circling over their fallen comrades. 'Where are you going?' one asked.

'I am taking these ten men as my bodyguard. We are going back for re-inforcements. We have a war on our hands.'

The Wild Dog who had been left in charge—a man who had been imprisoned for killing his wife and children in a drunken rampage—watched him go.

'The yellow-bellied bastard,' he spat out.

The twenty Wild Dogs did as they were bid. They might be the scum of the dungeons, but they were stout fellows. And they had a taste for killing. What were four *gringos* and a few Indians? They set off on foot, dodging from rock to rock along the mountainside.

Two hours later their innards, too, were being torn from them by the ravens and turkey vultures, who were hopping about squawking gleefully, having an unexpected feast. The *charros* had all been gradually cut down by arrow, lance, and rifle bullet. Soon there would be only a scattering of bleached bones to mark what had happened that day.

As Colonel Veraco and his men made their way back down the steep trails to the plain they passed through the ruined Yaqui village of Metallos. As their horses stepped through the deserted streets of smouldering burned houses a rock was hurled thudding into Veraco's back.

'Ach!' he shouted, ducking away. 'What was that?'

A woman bounded out of the ruins. She had been up on the mountain with her goats when her people had been rounded up for deportation. Her face was contorted in misery and she was wailing. 'My children, my sons, my parents, where have they gone? What have you done with them?'

In a frenzy she picked up more rocks, her wiry body contorted in fury, hurling them at the horsemen. One of the Wild

Dogs raised his revolver to kill her. A faint smile flickered on Veracos' lips, amused by the woman's insane bravery. He dodged his horse to avoid her flailing rocks. She was like a thing possessed, ducking down to find more ammunition. 'Leave her!' he ordered. 'Let her spread the word to other Yaquis what they can expect. We will be back for her.'

The little woman howled her grief and continued to bombard the horsemen as they cantered on their way. Veraco looked back and shouted. 'We will be back for all of you.' He hurried on as another stone nearly took his eye out.

'Cowards! Murderers!' she shouted.

The Yaquis were dancing their triumph, shuffling around the fire of *piñon* logs, their weird shadows flickering against the walls of the great cave, their bodies undulating back and forth, their voices a rhythmic unceasing ullulation as a muffled drum beat out.

Black Pete carved a hunk of horsemeat that was being roasted by Yaqui women on a spit, chawed at it, and grunted, 'They seem mighty pleased with themselves.'

'Let them have their moment,' Brother Francisco said, feeding scraps of meat to the little terrier in his lap. 'They have had too much to mourn. Their victory cannot last long, unless...'

'Unless what!'

'Unless the Mexican people rise up against their oppressors.'

'Yeah, I been wonderin' about that. Why do these *peons* take this kinda treatment? Anybody try to kick the American people about like that they would have a war on their hands.'

'Do you know how much the peon earns a day? The equivalent of eight of your cents. Eight cents! To feed his family on. Or try to feed them. The peons are half-starving. Some of them don't get paid at all. They are given tokens. They are virtual slaves of the rich *haciendados*. You *Americanos*, you see the peons sprawled in the shade under their sombreros and you say how quaint, what a pleasant life. Don't you see? They have no energy. No people whose diet consists of thin tortillas made of corn meal, flavoured to make it palatable with fierce chilli, are ever going to be likely to fight for a better life.'

'Yep,' Pete said. 'I bin feelin' a trifle peaky myself since comin' here.'

'You are paying the price of our highly spiced food, coupled with an almost total lack of knowledge of hygiene. You have probably been drinking contaminated water.'

'Yup. I'm gonna stick to beer from now on. This ain't so bad.' He tipped back his tin mug full of a sweet white liquid, *pulque,* which the Indians made from cactus. The Yaquis had been handing it to their visitors. This vast cavern, Cajeme's hide-out high in the *arroyos,* an ancient dwelling place of their ancestors, seemed to be pretty well-stocked. Numerous women and children were also living here, smiling happily now as they watched the dancers. *'Salud!'*

'That is all the peon has, cactus juice. Can you blame him attempting to escape from his burdens by continually getting drunk? Cheap cigarettes, black coffee.

110

Most of them die from disorders of the intestines.'

'You don't say,' Pete muttered, rubbing his own guts. 'These people look pretty fit by comparison.'

'They are. They have a simple, but healthy life. They eat nuts, dried fruit, goats' cheese, mescal beans. They know how to look after themselves. They were content and peaceful before the greedy *mestizos* decided they wanted their land. They have been constantly humiliated. Did you know that some Indians are not even allowed to enter main towns?'

'Nope, I didn't know that. Seems like they've been handed a pretty poor deal.'

'Huh!' Brother Francisco exploded. 'Poor deal! I would weep for Mexico, were it not time to fight. Do you know, I, a Christian, I was glad to see you kill those men this afternoon. I rejoiced. A man like you could lead this fight.'

'Uh, uh.' Pete shook his head. 'How long can these Indians fight the might of the military? Five, ten years at the most?'

'But, if the ordinary people rose up, the

111

peons, in great numbers, like a tide, they could sweep the oppressor from power,' Francisco cried.

'A pretty thought.'

'That is the message I am going to preach from now. I am going to go back down to the plain and shout it out. Equality. A fair wage. Hospitals. Schools. Revolution. Mexico is a rich country, but the wolves are taking its riches for themselves.'

'You reckon they goin' to allow you to preach that from the pulpit?'

'The pulpit? I have had enough of the pulpit. My church is one of the richest of the landowners. Diaz has returned a few of their monasteries to them, so now the priests are instructed to laud his name, to tell the peons what a great benevolent father he is to them. I am sick of lies. I will preach my message in the streets.'

'That might not be wise.'

'What is wise? Somebody has to start this work.'

'Hrmph!' Pete cleared his throat and took a swig of the late El Barracho's aguardiente which Miguel handed to him. 'How's your head?'

'Throbbing. But after this it will be throbbing more.' The bullet had creased Miguel's temple, knocking him unconscious for a short while. He had a bandage around his bald dome, and he grinned, 'Eh, *hombre*, I like the look of that li'l Indian lady.'

'Jest watch it,' Pete warned. 'We're guests.'

The earnest Brother Francisco was going on with his lecture. 'Did you know that the average Mexican lives for only twenty-seven years, less than under the Roman empire? That there is a twenty-five per cent infant mortality rate...?'

To change the subject Pete twiddled the terrier's long ears. 'Looks like he's got a bit of Chihuahua[1] in him? Bright-eyed little thing.'

'Perhaps, the bat ears. But otherwise he is what they call Jack Russell. He was left

---

[1] Chihuahua dogs were larger in those days.

behind by some rich English visitors to the hacienda. Or his mother was for giving birth. He was the runt of the litter. Weren't you, Ratty?' The dog gazed adoringly up at the priest. 'He would have been thrown out onto the street to join the other starving parish curs. I rescued him. Took him to live with the brothers. I had to get a special dispensation from the Pope, would you believe, for him to enter the monastery, to allow him to be fed meat. We are a vegetarian order, you understand?'

'You seem mighty fond of him—and him of you. I thought you Roman Catholics didn't believe in animals having souls.'

'Ratty has. Definitely. This little dog has more love and faithfulness, and, yes, courage, in him than any Mexican I have ever met. He is an honorary human. See, he can almost speak.'

Ratty gave a sneeze by way of agreement, grinned his little teeth up at Pete and began to scratch himself.

'Unfortunately,' the brother said, 'being human does not preclude his catching fleas.'

THIRTEEN

'Rider approaching!' The guard in the lookout tower above the great gates of the monastery began clanging his bell. 'Lone rider coming.'

Colonel Veraco ran into the courtyard and climbed up to the watch tower. He focused his field-glasses on the dark horseman coming out of the heat haze, coming at a steady lope across the plain of scrub and purple sage, straight-backed, almost military, the way he rode the big black stallion. 'It's the *Americano*,' he said, hardly able to believe his luck. 'What's that standard he's got in his hand?'

A blue flag, tattered and bullet-torn, flew proudly on the branch resting in the rider's rifle holster, blown out full by the rippling breeze as he charged straight as an arrow towards them, charging as if into battle. Upon the flag was a red St Andrew's cross and the thirteen stars of the secessionist States.

Ex-Lieutenant Pete Bowen had dug it out of his saddle-bag. Time to give the Bonny Blue an airing. If he was going to go—which seemed highly likely—he wanted to go in style. 'Wish I was in the land of cotton,' he was singing as he urged Jesus on towards the monastery. 'Wish I was in Dixie...hoorah, hoorah...I'll live an' die in...'

'Hold your fire,' Veraco shouted. 'Open the gates.'

Black Pete came galloping through, his standard of the True Confederacy rippling, and reined in as he circled the courtyard. He drew to a halt in front of Veraco. 'Howdy,' he called, touching his hat.

Nine Wild Dogs—the last of their breed—had their rifles and revolvers trained on him as Colonel Veraco bustled Pete through the stone corridors to the banqueting room. Don Ignatio looked up, milk dribbling from his lips, disturbed at his late breakfast. 'What's going on?' he quavered.

'It's the *gringo* traitor,' Veraco said, excitedly. 'He's come to surrender.'

'I ain't come to do nuthin' of the sort,' Pete said, standing before the long table as the Wild Dogs took up positions around him. 'What you talkin' about, traitor? We got captured by the Yaquis. All the others got wiped out.'

'It's a lie. He helped kill the *rurales*,' Veraco cried. 'OK, Bowen, put those revolvers on to the table. Careful. One false move—'

'Sure,' Pete drawled, taking the guns out by finger and thumb and gently placing them on the oak table. 'This ain't friendly-like.'

'What shall we do with him, Colonel?' Don Ignatio asked, waving the serving wenches away.

'Waal,' Pete said, sprawling in a high-backed chair, and putting one boot on the table. 'You could start by offering me a cup of that coffee, and mebbe one of them see-gars.'

117

'You insolent—' Veraco began, raising the riding crop in his fist.

'Wouldn't do that if I were you,' Pete said. 'I got some information.'

'Information?' Don Ignatio echoed. 'What sort of information.'

'Like the whereabouts of Cajeme's hideout. Now about that coffee.'

'He's lying. It's a trick,' Veraco protested. 'Let me whip the information out of the dog.'

'Just a moment,' Don Ignatio said, indicating that a coffee should be poured. 'Let us hear what he has to tell us.'

'Lyin' or not,' Pete said, striking a match on his thumb and lighting the Havana, 'I know where the hideout is. I been there. But, if you whipped me to the bone there's no way I could tell you in words. Too complicated. Mmm. Very nice see-gar.'

Veraco stamped his foot, impatiently, and looked around at his men. Now the Texan was unarmed they had relaxed their postures. 'How much do you want, you villain?' he shouted.

'Now you're talking. I sure could lead

you there. You got any reinforcements yet?'

'Not yet,' Don Ignatio blurted out. 'They are on their way from Navajoa. They should be here in three or four days' time.'

'Then, gents,' Pete said, sipping at his coffee, 'we might as well relax and wait for them. Any of you know how to play poker?'

'We were talking money,' Colonel Veraco said. 'You get two thousand dollars, *if* you come back with Cajeme's head.'

'Make it a thousand dollars on account. I sure don't trust you shit-faces.'

'First,' Colonel Veraco snapped, 'I'm going to have the pleasure of working you over.'

A small Remington derringer .38, with a three and a half-inch barrel appeared in Pete's hand from his boot holster. It had five chambers. He fired at the four nearest Wild Dogs, cutting them to pieces. He slipped down on his knees behind the table, his long arm grasping to retrieve a .44. He rolled away and fanned it at

119

three other *charros* by the door who were blazing away at him with their revolvers. They went spinning in their death agonies, blood and bone spattering the wall.

Lead tore searing through his left shoulder from the gun of a man to one side. 'Aighee!' Pete screamed, but twisted, and sent a .44 slug up through his attacker's chin, spilling out his brains. There was one Wild Dog left. He was attempting to back out of the door to raise the alarm. Pete's last bullet took his hair off.

The so-called Wild Dogs were either dead, or crawling and moaning, clutching their scrambled lungs or smashed ribs. One was dragging his broken hindquarters. Veraco had unbuttoned his shiny holster and had his revolver half-out. Pete looked up at him, pointed the Smith and Wesson at his trousers. 'I wouldn't,' he said. 'I might just have one slug left for your manhood.'

Veraco hesitated and slowly extended his arms high. Pete painfully got to his feet, pointed the heavy revolver at him. Veraco's eyes fluttered. There was a click.

'Wrong! It's empty. But I still got one in my li'l derringer. Always believe in havin' a side-gun.'

He cast an eye at Don Ignatio who was sat petrified in his chair amid the choking coils of gunsmoke, staring glassily at the dying men. 'What do you want?' he asked, hoarsely.

'You'll find out,' Pete said, carefully reloading his .44 from his belt and putting the twin pearl-handles back in his holsters, butts forward, the derringer returned to his boot. He pressed an arm to his left shoulder where blood was beginning to seep from his shirt and forced a thin grin. 'Li'l fugger tried to kill me.'

He heard shouts and men running and went to lock the door of the banqueting room with its great key. 'You're coming with me, Don Ignatio. Git to your feet.'

He prodded the old *haciendado* towards a side door that led to the kitchens. As he did so he turned and crashed a bullet into Veraco's knee, making him howl and collapse to the floor. 'A quick death's too good for you,' he snarled. 'I'll be back.

One of these nights I'll be there. Mark my words.'

He pushed Don Ignatio through the vast kitchens, winking at Miguel's fat lady as he did so. 'Is she still there?' his eyes asked. Her dark ones replied to his with an affirmative smile. She had been taking food to Louisa and attending to her bodily needs. To see the humiliation of Don Ignatio was something they had all silently longed for for years.

The round-shouldered old gentleman in his military uniform ambled on before him. 'Where are we going to?' he whined.

'You'll find out.'

Two *charros* appeared at the end of a corridor. Pete pulled Don Ignatio before him as a shield, sent lead whistling their way. They scampered for cover.

'Reckon this is the one,' Pete grunted, as he saw the spiral staircase and dragged the old man up behind him. He kicked open the door of the small store-room and saw Louisa's pale, anxious face, her luminous eyes beneath her wild shock of hair.

'I heard shooting. Are you all right?'

'Maybe I am. Maybe I'm not,' Pete whispered, holding his shoulder. 'Main thing's to get you outa here.'

'*Valgame Dios!*' she cried, going to him, raising her hands to his face. '*Mi amor.* Don't die on me now.'

'I'll try not to.' Pete gave a twisted grin, an emptiness in his insides. 'Though I ain't feelin' too hot. This ole rat's Don Ignatio. Meet Louisa Varga, you old lecher. The one you aimed to have as your unofficial virgin bride. The one whose father you had killed.'

Louisa gave a sob. 'The woman told me about that.'

'I didn't want him to,' Don Ignatio whimpered. 'I told him not to. What are you going to do with me?'

'You're our passport out of here. Come on. Move.'

'They will shoot you down,' Don Ignatio said.

'They can try.'

Cautiously they emerged into the court-yard. Men were posted around the walls, their rifles raised. Pete and Louisa backed away behind Don Ignatio in his magnificent uniform, a revolver at his head.

'Don't shoot, *charros*,' the old man pleaded.

Grooms stepped hurriedly out of the way as they reached the stables. 'Saddle Excellency,' Pete snapped.

The groom's eyes showed fear, but widened even more as the Smith and Wesson prodded his nose. He edged, hesitantly, into the stall. There was a banging and a crashing of hooves against walls, a whirling and clattering and whinnying. But, eventually the peon appeared, smiling, dragging the white stallion out.

In spite of his throbbing wound, and the giddiness in his head, Pete clambered into the saddle on to the fine horse. Excellency stomped and snorted and backed sideways and forwards. Pete held on hard with his good arm, soothed him and calmed him, and gradually brought him under control.

The peon whistled with admiration. 'What a horseman!'

'Get up behind me,' Pete ordered the *haciendado*. He put his good arm down to haul him up. 'Hang on to the stirrup, Louisa. Make a grab for Jesus as we go past.'

'But the gates are closed,' she protested.

'You wanna stay and be his bride?' He emerged into the courtyard and fired three fast shots at the watching *charros* making them duck down.

Outside the gates a young woman in a shawl and skirt, riding a burro, ambled forward. She jumped from the donkey when she heard the shots. She ran straight as a die towards the big gates, took a bundle of dynamite from her shawl, lit the short fuse, and ran back again.

There was a blistering crash and a roar as the gates tumbled down, dust and splinters billowing out.

'Come on,' Pete yelled and nudged the magnificent Arab stallion forward. He waited, whirling on the horse, a revolver at the ready, as Louisa quickly untied Jesus and leaped into the saddle. He dug in his spurs and they went flying away, hanging low, charging out of the monastery. None of the *charros* dared shoot too close for fear of hitting Don Ignatio. As they neared a peon woman in her shawl they slowed their pace and Melody smiled and jumped up behind Louisa.

They went soaring away across the purple plain, the two stallions neck and neck, their hooves thundering, their tails streaming in the breeze, the Bonny Blue flag proudly flying.

When they had put five miles between them Pete hoicked his good elbow back into Don Ignatio's guts. The old man tumbled into the sand. 'They can have him back now,' he said. 'He's kinda slowing me down.'

The old general lay on his back watching as his virgin and his horse disappeared over the horizon. A terrible helpless torment at their loss churned in his heart.

'Who is this man?' he wondered, awe in his voice.

FOURTEEN

'Go on without me,' Black Pete murmured.

The loss of blood and the pain of the bullet lodged in his shoulder had made him almost fall from his horse with a mind-spinning dizziness and nausea that came over him. He had tumbled forward hanging around the strong arched neck of Excellency.

Melody looked anxiously behind them. They had covered another ten miles since leaving Don Ignatio. There was no sign of any dust cloud on the plain, no sign of pursuit. Perhaps, when the *charros* found Don Ignatio they had merely returned with him to the hacienda. The thirty or so *charros* were, after all, only ordinary cowboys, not ruthless fighters. The Wild Dogs had been wiped out. Perhaps Don

Ignatio would wait until the military arrived, or until more scum of the prisons had been recruited before coming to look for them. It was a big 'perhaps'. She peered forward towards the *barrancas* and *cañons* of the distant mountains, their purple saw-tooth pattern harsh against the sky and slipped from the back of Jesus.

'I will tie him to the saddle before he falls,' she told Louisa as she darted across to catch at the Arab's reins. After the long hard gallop the elegant stallion was breathing hard and easier to handle. She took Pete's lariat and lashed his boots to the stirrups, and his body to the stallion's neck. He was semi-conscious and muttered, 'Go. Leave me.'

Melody hoisted herself up behind him and reached for the reins. The Arab danced and swirled but did not protest too much. 'We must find somewhere we can hide.'

'How about that clump of rocks,' Louisa suggested, after they had gone some way, pointing to an outcrop clothed with manzanita trees, their red bark and thick green leaves glowing in the rays of the setting sun. 'Will they see us there?'

'If we don't get that bullet out of him he will die. If they catch us they will surely kill him. So it is in the hands of God. You had better pray to our Lady of Guadalupe. As for us'—she smiled at the girl—'we will probably suffer a fate worse than death!'

They unleashed Black Pete and tried to help him to the ground as gently as possible, dragging him into the shade. Melody took his razor-sharp knife with its vicious point and cut open his shirt. 'We will need hot water,' she said. 'Can you make a fire?'

Louisa's own face was ashen with fear as she searched for kindling, took Pete's matches and blew a flame to life. She filled a canteen with water and put it on the fire to boil. At the same time she dampened his bandanna and gently dabbed at the tall outlaw's weatherbeaten brow. *'Querido mio,'* she murmured.

Melody gave her a curious look. Did Pete, she wondered, have the same tender feeling for her? He was a man almost twice the girl's age, hardened and cynical from a life of constant fighting and wandering. But, she had more important things to think about. She prised the casing from a bullet and sprinkled the gunpowder around the wound. She sterilized the knife in the by now boiling water.

'Hold him down,' she said to Louisa and pushed a bullet between Pete's teeth. 'This is going to hurt like hell.'

He half-opened his eyes and nodded, gripping his teeth hard on the bullet. Melody probed the knife into the wound. He gave a spasm of agony as steel cut into nerves, but Lousia hung on to him. Melody bit her lip and forced herself to cut into the flesh of the shoulder. 'It's lodged against the bone,' she said, and gasped with relief as she got the lead slug out.

Blood was flowing profusely. 'Give me a match,' she said. She lit it from the fire and touched it to the gunpowder, which went off with a fizzling flash. 'That's to cauterize it,' she explained. 'We won't be able to move him for a while.'

'Will he be all right?' Louisa asked.

'Well, I don't know. Like I said, it's up

to our Lady of Guadalupe.'

Melody took off her poncho and her blouse, her large melon-ripe breasts hanging loose. She tore the blouse into strips and bandaged the wound. 'What we need is a poultice of linseed and milk. But that is asking the impossible.'

They lay on either side of the man, who was muttering incomprehensibly in a state of fever, and watched the sun go down on the plain, and the first stars prick on. They expected any moment to see a band of *charros* appear seeking vengeance, but all was silent. A movement in the rocks startled Louisa, but it was only a kangaroo rat, looking oddly like that Australian creature, although much smaller, his nose twitching curiously, staring at them, forelegs raised, through red fire-reflecting eyes. He was not used to people sleeping in his rocks.

The drumbeat of hooves made Melody jump with alarm from her half-sleep. It was early dawn. She hugged her poncho around, for it was chill, and peered from the rocks. A stream of riders were approaching. She took one of Pete's Smith and Wessons and handed the other to Louisa, who was also awake and intently listening.

Suddenly Melody realized that the riders were coming from the direction of the mountains and she recognized the leading one, her own *querido mio*—Nathan. She rose, whistled and waved, excitedly.

He swerved towards her, followed by Miguel, Cajeme and several of the Yaqui Indians on the horses once belonging to *rurales* and Wild Dogs. Nathan jumped from his saddle and said, 'We thought you were all dead.'

'Pete near is.'

Melody put an arm around the cowboy's neck, kissing him, as he peered down at his friend. 'I got the bullet out but...'

'You done well, honey. I should never have let you two go off on your own.'

'Pete told me before he passed out that soldiers will be here in three or four days,' Melody said. 'Don Ignatio is probably waiting for them before he comes in pursuit. That's his horse. Isn't he a beauty?'

'He sure is.'

'And this is Louisa, the girl he went looking for.'

'So is she,' Nathan smiled. 'A real Spanish beauty. He certainly knows how to choose 'em. Horses and gals.'

'Hey, more beautiful than me?'

'No,' he grinned, hugging her. 'Nobody could be more beautiful than you.'

Cajeme was standing beside them, his dark, aquiline face solemn. 'You say three or four days' time soldiers come?'

'Si.'

'We camp here. We wait for other warriors to come. Tonight we attack fort.'

'You know, that ain't a bad idea.' Nathan tipped his Stetson back and scratched at his blond thatch. 'Could be that Don Ignatio has sent what *charros* he's got left to patrol the frontier. He probably thinks that us *gringos* will try to get back to Arizona where he wouldn't be able to touch us.'

'I blew up the gate with the dynamite

you gave me. Hey, *bueno!* We will be able to walk in.'

'We?' Nathan echoed. 'I ain't letting you risk your purty li'l neck again.'

She kissed and hugged the cowboy. 'You try and stop me. I have a debt to settle with Don Ignatio.'

Louisa gripped Nathan's sleeve, her eyes dark and trembling as a startled doe's. 'Will Pete be all right.'

'That ole bastard! People bin tryin' to hang him and kill him for years. He's as tough as saddle leather. He'll pull through.'

Later in the day the warriors on foot arrived, accompanied by Brother Francisco leading his *burro*, the little dog—*pequeno perro*—trotting before them, his long ears alert, his tail wagging furiously.

'I have just what you need for a poultice in my pack,' Francisco cried, kneeling beside Pete. 'Let me attend to him. I got a gourd of goat's milk from the last village we passed.'

'He has lost a lot of blood,' Louisa said.

'Ah, that is nothing to a man like him. I will make a stretcher for him from these trees and drag him behind my *burro* back to the mountains. He will be back in the saddle in a week or two.'

'I prayed all night to the Lady of Guadalupe. She has answered me.'

Francisco smiled at her, curiously. 'I believe that may well be, my child. This is a good man. He defends the weak, rescues the innocent. Our Lady wanted him to live.'

FIFTEEN

It was nearly midnight when the Yaquis, led by Cajeme, Nathan and Miguel, attacked the hacienda. They did so stealthily, leaving their horses in the curiously shaped hills behind the former monastery, creeping through the brakes of bamboo, across the fields, past the flimsy huts of the peons. The lookout did not see them. He knew nothing, only the burning pain of an arrow as it pierced his chest. It was as Nathan had surmised. Most of the *charros* had been sent off to patrol the frontier 200 miles to the north, expecting the *Americanos* to make a break for home. Only a dozen had been left behind to act as bodyguard to their master. Nobody had anticipated another audacious attack. What *charros* there were were playing their guitars around their campfire in the courtyard, or flirting with the servant girls in the kitchens. They hardly had time to shout a warning, to draw their revolvers as arrows, lances and knives cut them down.

It was a warm humid night after a day in which the temperature had soared over the 100°F mark. Don Ignatio had dined well on roast lamb, washed down by a bottle of vintage wine and a few glasses of brandy. He felt none the worse for his adventure. In fact, he felt amazingly randy, considering that he was nearly seventy-five. It was so humid he decided it would be lovely to cool off in his bathing pool tended by the gentle hands of his three favourite serving girls. He rang a little silver bell and summoned them to follow him.

Only one bodyguard accompanied him, a trusted *charro* who, in his huge sombrero and tight embroidered suit, lounged against a wall of the little oasis and watched, with a lick of envy, Don Ignatio's withered naked limbs floating amid his dark, glistening girls, who sported about him like seals.

137

Suddenly another girl appeared, a pretty little *muchacha,* her cheeks the colour of ripe peaches, her hair glistening blue-black. She strolled forward to the poolside and smiled at Don Ignatio and slowly, teasingly pulled off her poncho to reveal an exquisite body, her deep breasts pushing firmly out to two dark rounded aureoles about the pert nipples.

Don Ignatio, and, indeed, the guard, licked their lips, their eyes rivetted. 'Hello, my dear,' the *haciendado* purred up to her. 'Where have you come from? I haven't seen you before, have I?'

The girl smiled, mysteriously, standing there in only her thin cotton skirts, hands akimbo, her breasts thrust out.

'Please, my sweet one.' Don Ignatio extended his reedy arms to her, his gold teeth glinting, his mouth almost watering in expectation of her touch. 'Please come to me.'

'I thought I would find you here, Don Ignatio.' The well-endowed young beauty began to lower herself into the pool. 'They tell me you like virgins.'

'Yes, yes,' he begged, as she put out her hands to touch his shoulders, floating out with him into the deep water. 'Please.'

The guard shrugged bitterly, lit a cigarette and turned away. He could not bear to watch. How did the old devil manage it? What it was to have money, to crook your finger and have any girl you wished. Ai-yai-yaiee!

'I have come to avenge those virgins. I have come to avenge all the men you had flogged, the people of Honi you massacred,' Melody murmured to him. 'I have come to kill you.'

Don Ignatio could not believe his ears. What was going on? She was pressing herself down upon him; she was stifling him with her breasts; she was pushing him under the water; he could not breathe; could not cry out; he was kicking his legs and flapping his arms for all he was worth, but she was holding him. He was choking; he was going weak; he was looking up through the water at her relentless eyes as her strong arms dominated him. Everything was becoming blurred. I am dying, he thought.

'I hope you rot in hell,' Melody hissed as she saw the old man cease his twitchings and sink to the bottom of the pool, lying there.

The serving girls screamed and splashed away from her in horror. The guard rushed forward, his rifle at the ready. Astonishment crossed his face as he registered what had happened. He raised the rifle to his shoulder and aimed at Melody, who tried to bob down beneath the water's surface. 'You bitch!'

'I wouldn't do that,' Nathan shouted.

The guard spun around on his high-heeled boots to see the Texan standing in the doorway, an old Navy Colt in his fist. The guard fired the rifle with a rapid jerking movement as the Colt belched flame. Its lead pierced the Mexican's aorta, sent him tumbling into the pool. He lay there in a hazy cloud of blood.

Melody surfaced, shook the water from her hair, and called, 'Thank goodness you turned up. Why don't you come in? It's nice in here.'

'With two corpses? No thanks! Euk! Why do you keep giving me these scares?'

Melody pulled herself out and stood on the flagstones, dripping water, her arms over her breasts, and stared sullenly at the dead bodies. 'Do you remember that day we watched them bury the Indians alive and ride over them smashing their skulls? I vowed then to kill the man responsible. To kill him with my bare hands.'

'Whewee!' Nathan whistled, pulling her into his arms. 'You're quite a gal.'

In the cellars of the old monastery Miguel was laughing as he guzzled one of Don Ignatio's rare vintage red wines, and nuzzled and groped his fat lady cook. There were hundreds of bottles. 'How are we going to take them all?' he cried, as he smashed off the neck of another bottle to sample it.

'You could take one of the peon's wagons. Look at those lovely hams and sausages hanging there. Don't they make your mouth water? How about a side of beef? Give you plenty of strength and stamina. You'll be needing that with me along.'

'Eh?' Miguel grunted. This was news to him. 'What about your husband?'

'Ach. I want a real man.'

'Let me roll out one of these kegs and give it to the peons. Time for a fiesta before we head back to the mountains.'

'They wouldn't touch it. They are whipped dogs.'

'*Caramba!* We will soon see. But first—'

After he had had his way with her over a barrel, he rolled it out to the courtyard. Someone had whispered to the peons what was going on and they had hurried from their homes, crowding silently into the courtyard to stare at the Yaquis and the *gringos*, who were loading a wagon with food and wine and cigars, with guns and bullets, and silverware from the mansion.

One of the Yaquis danced out into the courtyard wearing the uniform coat of Generalissimo Don Ignatio, covered with gold and scarlet braiding and decorations. He grinned at them, thrusting the general's sword threateningly. Another, a tall graven-faced one, surely Cajeme himself, had girdled his waist with Don Ignatio's scarlet sash.

A whisper went through the solemn watching peons that Don Ignatio was dead, killed by that young girl, drowned in his own swimming pool, and there was an awed hush.

A wild bald-domed *vaquero* staggered out, laughing, rolling a barrel. *'Vino!'* he shouted. 'Come, drink. You have much to celebrate. Go inside, take what food you want. It is fiesta time!'

He picked up an axe and smashed into the barrel. The wine gushed out like blood over the cobblestones, but not one peon stepped forward to drink from it.

'These men will surely hang,' a mother hissed at her children.

'After their backs have been flogged,' another said. 'As for that girl—'

Some even crossed themselves at fear of reprisals. The *rurales* would come...

'Have you no guts?' Miguel roared. 'Come drink, eat, you sheep.'

But the peons merely stared as the invaders loaded the cart with Don Ignatio's priceless belongings, harnessed his fine horses, parted for them as they rode off into the night.

SIXTEEN

A pack of wolves surrounded Black Pete as he lay beside his campfire. They were preparing to attack, their fangs glistening, their tongues lolling, their foetid breath in his face. Any second they would tear him apart. He struggled and shouted to fight them off...

When he came out of his fever on the fourth day he saw that they were not wolves but Yaquis, sat around in the great cavern, the flames' reflections splashing on the walls. Or, perhaps his wolf had been the little dog that scratched at him and peered into his face. He closed his eyes and went spinning away again, away into memories of his life, images of bodies bloated like hogs in the fields of Shiloh, of climbing through the snows across Bear

Mountain pursued by vigilantes, of the spine-chilling voodoo mass he had witnessd in the black township of Devil's Creek when he caught up with Blue Jay, of his Cherokee Confederate soldiers hunted down and hanged from the trees, of cattle trails and flooded rivers and droughts, and the faces of men he had killed, of the noose burning around his own neck, and his wife, for whom he had held no bitterness, being devoured with her lover in the flames of his ranch home. Abilene and Dodge City, Santa Fe, the outlaws' hangout at Old Fort Sumner, New Mexico, and the shoot-out with Billy the Kid and his boys at Windy Flats. So many faces, so many gunfights, so many deaths.

The Yaquis painted a sand drawing of religious symbols and they dragged him over to lay him in the centre, and squatted around him chanting a mournful dirge, as the *Brujo,* their medicine man, flicked him with his wand and summoned the help of the underworld to give him back life and make him strong. They believed that the first people had come up from under the ground and they had been given the sacred duty to protect the land, to reign over the animals, who would give them their food and clothing and tools...

But a great lethargy was upon Pete as he heard them chanting, and he was dragged back into the past. He resurfaced from his dreams days later and saw the Mexican girl sitting quietly nearby praying as she touched her rosary beads. There was something about the shadowed cut of her cheek, the mass of her hair that was both dignified and proud for one so young. She turned languorous, watchful eyes to him and saw that he had awakened. As he reached out a hand to her she gave him a joyful smile.

'Louisa!' he said, thinking she was his wife. 'You've come back.'

'Yes, I won't leave you,' the girl whispered, her cool hand gently touching his brow. 'I think it is you who has been on a long journey and come back to me.'

Her touch was like a blessing to him. 'I thought I was seeing things. I thought you were my wife.' He forced a grin and put a hand up to touch her face. 'You ain't. But you sure look mighty like her when she was young.'

'First you think we are wolves. Now you think I am your wife,' Louisa laughed. 'No, I'm not. But maybe I will be.'

'Maybe,' he grunted, but he still felt too weak from loss of blood to say much. His shirt was sticky with sweat, his thick hair grimy and tangled from his fever. 'Jeez. I could do with a wash.'

'There is a mountain stream outside. Maybe'—and she put an arm under him and helped him hobble out of the cavern—'you must not do too much. We do not want the wound to open.'

The blaze of sunshine and blue sky hit him like a lightning flash. It was like returning to life after darkness. 'I thought I was a goner,' he murmured as she took the soiled clothes from him and tenderly washed him in the stream. She dried him and helped him into a clean sun-dried shirt, like a nurse.

'You must eat to get your strength back,' she said.

Pete broke an orange into segments and bit into its clean, clear juice. The taste struck him like the most beautiful fruit he had ever tasted. 'It sure is strange to be back,' he said. 'Let's sit here in the sunshine awhile.'

'Aih! *Amigo!*' Miguel waved a wad of notes under Black Pete's nose. 'I found the key to Don Ignatio's safe. Fifty thousand pesos here. You were right. This is better than any silver mine.' He shook a bag of silver and jewellery. 'Look at these. We are rich. It's time we headed out of here.'

The Yaquis had returned in triumphant mood. More and more people were deserting their villages to join them in the mountains. They were celebrating with Don Ignatio's rare vintages, drunkenly wailing for their dead children at the same time. Sensibly they stored the hams and sides of beef they had pillaged from the monastery in the cavern for future use. They melted down the silverware. And busied themselves making flint arrowheads, examining the *rurales'* captured rifles, preparing for war.

'This war is no business of ours.' Miguel's voice was as harsh as a raven's croak. 'We must get out while we can.' He had slipped the clutches of his fat mistress and was eager to be away, free as a bird. 'When will you be fit to ride?'

'Pretty soon,' Pete said, glancing up at the mountains towering over them. 'I want to get Louisa to safety. There's no life for her back there.'

Miguel stood before him in his purple serape, what was left of his hair flailing about his shoulders in the wind. His Buntline was tucked into the thick leather belt around his waist. 'The soldiers are coming. There is no way the Yaqui can win.'

'Cajeme will fight for his land,' Melody put in. 'There is nothing else he can do.'

Nathan produced a rough map on waxed cloth from his saddle-bag. 'Cajeme says we should go. He has offered a man to guide us through the mountain passes. We should be able to get through to'—he jabbed his finger—'there, the Lake de Los Patos. Then we can either trail on down south along Doniphan's route to Chihuahua, or head east for Eagle Pass and back into Texas.'

'I do not like to run away while the man who killed my father still lives.' Louisa's eyes burned fiercely. 'Do you say Veraco was not at the monastery?'

'Nope. He'd quit the coop.'

'Yeah, I shoulda put a bullet in his heart,' Pete brooded, darkly. 'I made a mistake there. But, you're right. It's time to go. I want you four to go on without me. I'll catch up.'

'We ain' goin' nowhere,' Nathan said, 'without you, *amigo.*'

SEVENTEEN

News had reached the governor's residence in Sonora that 250 Yaqui prisoners had committed joint suicide, leaping overboard into the ocean from the ship that was transporting them, mothers holding their children under the waves until they had drowned.

'That is typical of them,' Ramón Corral complained, moodily. 'They just wanted to cheat us out of our bounty.'

'You can't trust them. It will be better when they are all dead,' Colonel Ferdinand Veraco agreed.

'And whose fault is it Cajeme and his warriors are not dead? Yours, for hiring those *gringos*.'

Veraco groaned at the pain in his wounded knee, and at the memory of

152

the *Americano*. 'Don't worry, Ramón. I have scoured the State prisons and found many men ready to fight for us. You will have your *rurales* and I more Wild Dogs. Next time there will be no mistakes.'

'Next time! *Rurales!* Wild Dogs! I am sending the military in. They will rake through the Yaqui valley, through the mountains. No Yaqui, no *gringo* bandit will escape. And don't call me Ramón. To you I am your Excellency. I would like to know why you so quickly ran away and left Don Ignatio to his fate? Sometimes I think you are chicken.'

'I had to warn you... Your Excellency, report what had happened.'

'How come this outlaw didn't kill you! Maybe this is all a trick? Maybe you are in league with him to share Don Ignatio's loot?'

'Don't be absurd. Look at my knee. I can hardly walk. I had to be brought here in Don Ignatio's coach. I don't know why.' He shuddered at the memory of Black Pete's threat. 'He is a strange man.'

'Huh! From now on you liaise with

the military. You get out there, Colonel. You get after him. You kill him and you bring back that fine horse, that Spanish girl. She will make me a true aristocrat. Understand? Otherwise you will no longer be my *jefe*. I will break you, Colonel.'

'Yes, Your Excellency.'

'I am posting rewards of a thousand pesos for the heads of the two *gringos*, for the girl who killed Don Ignatio, and for the Mexican who rides with them.'

'*Bueno*,' Veraco said, leaning on his cane. 'I will claim them all. You will see.'

More bad news arrived the next day at the governor's palace. A terrible earthquake had reduced Bavispe, to the south of the province, to rubble. The military had been diverted from fighting the Yaqui to digging through the ruins, rescuing survivors. The 'Great Father', *El Presidente*, had to show the Great Powers that he was concerned about his people.

'It will be weeks before the troops get here,' the governor moaned. 'All these

154

delays. Even God is conspiring against us.'

Veraco, who had been summoned before him, dusted off his new *kepi* and smiled, insidiously. 'Don't worry, Your Excellency. I will settle this without military help. You will see. Have I a free hand?'

'Burn their villages, destroy their crops. Make the whip sing. It is the only language they understand. These new Wild Dogs—they are good men?'

'The best. They would murder their own sister for a few pesos. Which reminds me, that idea of yours of a reward for Yaqui ears, I don't think it will work.'

'Why?' the governor asked.

'There isn't a lot of difference between the ears of a Yaqui and those of a peon. The bodies of numerous peons have been found—earless. The landowners are complaining. I fear my Wild Dogs have been trying to earn a little extra.'

Ramón roared with laughter, his body shaking so his silver conchos jingled like bells. 'Good for them. That is the spirit of enterprise I like. But, OK, make it seven dollars for a Yaqui scalp.'

'We used to be able to get three hundred for an Apache's.'

'These are not Apache. The Apache were a scourge in the side of Mexico for four centuries. These Yaqui won't give us much more trouble. By the way, what is happening to Don Ignatio's estate?'

'His two sons are returning from their studies in America. They can carve it up between them,' the *jefe* said. 'I only hope they don't bring back any of these crazy ideas about democracy. It won't work in Mexico. As you say, Ramón, all a peon understands is the whip.'

The governor surlily swiped all the paperwork from his great desk, put his boots up, lit a cigar and uncorked a bottle of aguardiente. 'You don't know all the trouble I have,' he shouted, 'with these affairs of state. Don't let me down, Colonel. I want the heads of those four *renegados*. Be off with you.'

Veraco's knee was too painful to click his boot heels, but he saluted smartly. 'Trust in me, Your Excellency.' But, there was only one head he thirsted for. That was the head of Black Pete.

Cajeme's darkly wooden face rarely broke into a smile. A savage solemn mask, it bore the burden of his people's woes. But, sometimes, as he sat and spoke to Black Pete he showed himself, beneath his rage, to be a gentle person. 'There are two worlds,' he said. 'The timeless people, the holy ones from the underworld, and us, the people in time. Wherever we go we remember that the holy people are everywhere, in everything. We must connect with the spirits—us surface people—if we are to live truly.'

'How do you square that with these Mexicans trying to wipe you out?'

'They have no holiness. They are confused. They inflict their greed and suffering on us, but we will survive. By nature we Yaqui are not a warlike people. We like to live our life lightly, to be like the humming bird, to draw our strength from the cactus and desert, to live with the outside beauty inside us, to be at ease with the holy people. It is not our nature to kill, but I fear we have to. They have pushed us to the cliff edge.'

His *brujo* was not so optimistic, however, and warned, 'I see the future. It is dark with blood. We will all die or see bondage.'

'If we die in battle it is good,' Cajeme replied. 'It is good to die for our land.'

Black Pete kept his own counsel. These people had offered the hand of peace to their oppressors and had been treated with evil. In spite of everything Cajeme still believed in the goodness of life. Pete felt guilty to be planning to pull out.

As the days passed, and he began to exercise and move about, while Miguel and Nathan were away on scouting expeditions with the Yaquis, he often spoke to Brother Francisco.

'You're looking better, Pete,' Francisco laughed. 'But with Louisa's devoted nursing, the Yaquis making their magic for you, and Our Lady of Guadaloupe cheering us on there was no way you couldn't pull through.'

'Well,' Pete smiled, 'I know Louisa's

religious. But, I can't claim to be. My Ma made me study the Bible but I ain't a believer in the Creation. I'm more inclined to agree with this feller Darwin that we came up from the apes; that it's the survival of the fittest; that man has a killer instinct.'

'There is Good and Evil,' Brother Francisco said. 'It is up to good men to fight Satan and his minions.'

'Now you *sound* like a priest. But, to git back to the Creation. One day me and Jesus was ridin' through the woods in Arizona and we came out on this rim of a vast cañon. Eight miles wide and a mile deep. Jeez, talk about awesome. We nearly went into it. The Grand Cañon, of course. Only nobody had bothered to remind us it was there. Guess they thought we was aware of it. Somethun's sure happened here,' I said to Jesus. 'And it weren't done in no seven days. Later, I was reading in a newspaper about some professor who reckoned the Colorado river began eroding through those cliffs in the Plasticine age a million years ago.'

'Pleistocene, I think, is the word,' Brother Francisco, who had studied much, corrected.

'Yeah, and I saw one of them great condors gliding over the *cañon*, a strange black bird with a white head and ten-foot wing span, its feathers spread like fingers. That bird's been around a long, long time.'

'True. Similiar ones were found, I read, in a California tar pit along with a sabre-toothed tiger. Certainly, these modern discoveries shake a man's faith. But, to me, it all testifies to the greater glory of God. We simply cannot take the Bible too literally any more.'

Ratty, who was draped over his master's knee, clinging warmly to him, pricked his ears up, his eyes bright, an attentive listener to all this.

When he was more back on his feet, Pete took his bedroll to lay out on the mountainside in the moonlight. He felt more at home under the stars. He was rolling a cigarette one night when Louisa climbed up to join him. She pulled his shirt open to examine his wound. 'It is healing nicely,' she said, and her fingers fluttered down his strong chest, down to his muscled abdomen, marvelling at the other bullet marks, the rope burn around his throat. Her inquisitive fingers were gentle but exciting. She straddled him, her legs bare beneath her skirt. He eased her blouse down to admire her ivory-pearl body in the moonlight, and nuzzled her warm breasts. Her mass of black hair hung over his eyes as she murmured, 'I think you are strong enough now, *querido mio.*'

'I thought you wanted to be married.'

'There will be plenty of time for that,' she whispered as she took his face in her hands and kissed him.

EIGHTEEN

Every step that his horse took, jolting his wounded knee, burned like a fire of hatred in the *jefe politico*'s mind for the man who had shot him, the *Americano*. A desire for vengeance obsessed him. And a desire to rid himself of his fears, of the *gringo* appearing in the night to get him. He was nervous and irritable, unable to sleep, pushing his Wild Dogs up through a lesser-known *cañon*.

The small Yaqui village of Encenjenito seemed to hang in the crags, its adobe houses built into the cliff. Again there were only a few women and children and old men. The programme of deportations was going well as the *rurales* methodically worked their way along the Yaqui valley. He wanted information. Where was Cajeme?

The fools. Even though they were kicked and flogged by his men they sat cross-legged and mute, or lay, moaning, clinging to the earth as if it were a mother.

'We won't get anything out of them,' —Veraco snapped his fingers—'hang them all. It is tiresome, but it has to be done. Yes, the whole damned village. Everybody.'

The *viciosos*[1] laughed as a little Indian-woman was strung up, her heels kicking air, her neck snapping, her head forced to one side, as her mouth opened in its last agonised croak. She still had the small basket-like hat on her head that she had used for carrying bundles.

Soon bodies were hanging from the branches of the wind-blasted trees, some from door jambs. They were running out of places to hang them from, they were running out of rope. The Indians resolutely accepted their fate. Perhaps they believed they were going to a better world.

'They are stubborn fools,' Colonel

---

1   *viciosos*—bad men.

Veraco shouted to the Wild Dogs, who appeared to be enjoying the break. 'Shoot the rest. It is a waste of ammunition, I know. But, we haven't time to hang about'—he smiled, sardonically—'if you will forgive the joke.'

Black Pete had been giving Louisa some pointers on riding, how to hold herself, how to change from a canter to a lope, how to go with the horse. Excellency was magnificent, a horse like Alexander the Great might have ridden, graceful and footsure, he seemed to dance across the rocks, and the girl had a natural flow with him.

Louisa reined Excellency in and smiled radiantly down at Pete. 'Let me take him for a little ride,' she cried. 'He needs the exercise.'

'Waal, I don't know,'—Pete tugged at his moustache ends, uncomfortably—'it ain't safe.'

'Don't worry. Nobody will have got past Nathan and Miguel and the Yaquis. Just down to where the *cañon* begins. Please.'

'Waal'—But before he could reply Louisa had given the horse his head and gone rattling away in a flurry of hooves and harness. He watched her go and bit his lip. 'Damn,' he said. 'Damn ole fool I am.'

Louisa galloped across the plateau. It was such an exhilarating sensation to have the fine horse, his power, under her, that she strayed further and further away from the safety of the big cavern. She had only ever ridden an old donkey before. And she wanted to reach the edge of the plateau, to take a last look down across the *cañons* and mountain ranges at the plain, the land where she had lived all her life. It would be the last chance she would have of seeing it. Pete reckoned that tomorrow he would be fit enough to get on Jesus and move out.

There was nobody to be seen among the scattered white rocks on the table-top of the plateau. She followed a weaving goat path across it, reached the cliff edge, and tied the horse to a bush. She climbed down further so that she could get a view of the plain. Yes, that was her land away over there. And that the valley of the Yaqui below her. She could see a thin line of *rurales*, making their way up a trail, and she held her breath as she saw houses burning. The village of Encenjenito. They were getting near.

Startled, she jumped up as she heard the clatter of hooves behind her. *'Ole!'* a rough voice shouted. 'What have we here?' Louisa looked up to see a ring of Wild Dogs on horseback grinning at her. For seconds, it occurred to her to leap from the cliff, such was her desperation.

'What do you know! Don Ignatio's white stallion. And the beautiful Spanish girl. Colonel Veraco will be very pleased with us. What a catch!'

The *jefe politico*, indeed, was pleased. He, himself, tossed a rope around Louisa's slim neck, tightened it with a fierce jerk, and tied it to his saddle horn. He spurred his chestnut and started back down the precipitous mountain trail dragging Louisa on foot after him. He wanted to get back to the plain. He felt safer there than in the mountains. Excellency was led along behind the whooping Wild Dogs who had broken into a high-spirited filthy song directed at the girl's discomfiture. Like all Mexican songs it went on and on into successive spontaneous verses, intercut by a loud chanting chorus from the grinning horsemen. One occasionally flicked his whip at the girl to keep her going.

'Oh, *Valgame Dios!* What have I done?' she kept repeating. What a fool she was! Black Pete had risked his life twice before to rescue her and now, when all had looked so well for them, she had cast him again into mortal peril. For she knew he would not hesitate to come after her. The rocks cut her feet, the rope around her neck seared the flesh, her body and lungs ached from running. She tried to keep up with the horsemen for she knew if she tripped and fell it would be all up with her. They passed through the village of Encenjenito, the houses smouldering in ashes, bodies hanging from the trees, or lying sprawled in grotesque postures on the ground, shot in the head, a mother hugging her child to her. One, who was still not dead, lying among the fly-buzzing corpses, raised his hand, pleadingly, to them as they passed. The Wild Dogs laughed and cantered on down towards the Yaqui River.

Three of the *vaqueros* had been dispatched by the *jefe politico* up to the table-top of the plateau to ride under a white flag. They rode a good distance attempting to follow the girl's trail until it petered out. One of them fired off three rapid shots of his revolver and they waited, nervously. A man never knew where these Indians might be.

Black Pete heard the shots. They were not all that far off, heard their echoes reverberating through the harsh mountains. And his heart froze, as if it had ceased beating. Louisa! Why had he let her go? And it began again pulsating faster than normal. Cajemo, his warriors and Pete's *amigos* had been away for two days riding to guard their mountain bastion. And now it sounded like somebody had sneaked up behind him.

He pulled on his macinaw, and his hat low over his eyes, checked his revolvers and took his rifle, and, slowly, eased himself up on to the black stallion. 'Come on, Jesus,' he said, nudging his knees into him.

They cantered off away from the big cavern, the wind blowing fiercely chill at this altitude, iron-shod hooves reverberating as they passed through the great boulders. He saw the three Wild Dogs sitting their mustangs on a pinnacle point, their white flag fluttering. 'Damn!' he snarled, his worst fears realized. 'Damn their eyes. Damn their souls.'

A sickly smile crossed the face of one of the *vaqueros,* a thin man with jaws as thin as a wolf's, covered in black stubble. It was a wonder his mouth didn't water at the prospect of a kill as Pete reined in before them.

'Are you Black Pete Bowen, *señor?*'

'*Si.*'

'You know the village of Honi?'

'*Si.*'

'You come down there just after sun-up *mañana.* You surrender to the *jefe* alone, no guns, *comprende?*'

'*Si*. What then?'

'The girl goes free.'

'How can I be sure of that?'

'You have the *jefe's* word of honour, *sẽnor*, as an officer and a gentleman.'

Pete sat Jesus and watched them through narrowed eyes. He rolled some baccy in his mouth and spat out a quid of juice. 'Some word! But, I guess it's all we have.'

'That's all you have, *señor*. You come in, alone, unarmed. We have a nice comfortable cell ready for you.'

'What if I don't? I had other plans for tomorrow.'

'Change them, *señor*. Otherwise, you know what happens to the girl?'

'Tell me,'—and an emptiness filled Pete's chest for he could guess what they would say.

'The girl goes to us. As a reward for her capture. Not just us three. All of us Wild Dogs. What a beauty! What a time we will have. You think she is a virgin, *señor?*'

Pete stared at him, stone-faced, tempted to kill him now. 'I heard tell Ramón Corral wanted her for himself,' he whispered.

'Pah! The Colonel say that she is only a peon girl. The governor can have her when we are finished. *Comprende?*'

'Yeah, I get the picture. I wouldn't put anything past that low-bellied crawling scum-bug, Veraco. He ain't a man. He's a killing machine.'

The *vaquero* squealed with laughter, pushing his sombrero back as he leaned on his saddle horn. 'I will tell the Colonel your kind words.' He grinned at his companions. '*We* would prefer you didn't come down, eh? Much better for us Wild Dogs. Why don' you go back to gringoland? Why bother with this li'l girl?'

'Dogs is too good a name for you scum. I know a li'l dog who wouldn't even piss on you.'

'Haiya-yee!' The Mexicans howled with laughter. 'You got the message, *gringo*. Maybe we see you. Maybe we don't. Maybe the colonel doing things to that li'l girl right now. Eh?'

They dragged their mustangs around

and galloped away, their laughter trailing back to him.

'Damn their eyes. Damn their lies,' Pete muttered.

He felt meaner than a gut-shot grizzly.

NINETEEN

Her body was trembling with exhaustion from being dragged behind the horses. Her hair was unkempt and wind-blown, and her blouse was torn immodestly from the way the *vaqueros* had manhandled her, groping her body as they tumbled her into the *jefe*'s office. Well, not so much an office, more a half-burned house in the village of Honi where he had set up his table and chairs. The field outside was littered with grinning Yaqui skulls.

'If you co-operate we could be friends,' Colonel Veraco purred, in his icy way. 'The *Americano* Bowen will surrender here tomorrow. If you then show us the way to Cajeme's hide-out we will let him live. We will let you both ride out of here.'

'Lies,' she moaned, as she sprawled

collapsed on a chair, leaning her arms on the table. 'Why should I believe the snake who killed my father? Who massacred this village? I know all about you.'

Veraco snatched her by the hair and smashed her head down on to the table edge, screaming in her ear. 'You, *señorita*, could very easily lose your looks.'

'I am not *señorita*. I am *señora*. *Señora* Bowen. I am an American citizen now. You have no right to touch me.'

'What do you mean? How can you be?'

'Brother Francisco married us. Yesterday. Your president would not like you interfering with an American citizen. He needs us as his allies.'

'Ha!' Veraco slashed his riding quirt across her shoulders. 'Don't lie to me.'

'It's true,' she sobbed, trying to ease the rope around her lacerated neck.

'Huh! I wondered where that quarrelsome priest had got to. But'—he ran his fingers across her back to soothe her—'the same offer applies. You both go free. Clear off to America and good riddance.'

Louisa shrugged his fingers away. They made her feel creepy, like spiders all over her. The sting of his crop was preferable. 'Do you really think I would betray the Yaquis? I would rather die.'

'You will die if you don't, but slowly. First my Wild Dogs will have you while your'—he emphasized the word, sarcastically—'*husband* watches. You know what they like doing to a girl? They bite her tits off. They do horrible things with their whips. Oh, yes, they have hours of fun.'

'You are sick. All of you. Foul, sick, a disgrace to the name of Mexico.'

Colonel Veraco smiled and lit a cigarette. 'What a fine speech! For an ignorant peon. How dare you even breathe in my presence? Do you realize what I could do to you?' Veraco loved torturing her, not only physically, but mentally. It gave him an exquisite sense of power. Similar to that he had known as a child when pulling wings off beautiful butterflies. Yes, he would pull off her wings. He would kick her into the mire. And it added to his pleasure knowing she was a Creole. Only the top six per cent of the social elite in Mexico City had skins as fair as this. And knowing she was Bowen's slut. Maybe, if it were true, his wife? 'Would you like me to kill everybody in your father's village? That's what I will do if you don't co-operate.'

'Kill me. Kill everybody in Mexico. What are you'—she looked up at him, defiantly —'some kind of disease, some slime, sent to execute us all?'

Veraco's face froze, only his eyes flickering, like a snake's. He stabbed his burning cigarette down on to her hand. Louisa gasped and tried not to cry out as it burned into the flesh. It made a fizzling sound. A yellow bloody mark.

'Throw her into the cellar,' he shouted. 'Find some rats. Throw them in, too, for company.'

As they dragged her away, Louisa turned and hissed at the *jefe*, 'Pete will kill you for this.'

When she had gone Veraco shuddered, as if someone had stepped on his grave. He poured a drink, composed himself. No. The *gringo* would have no chance.

La Journada—the journey—life's journey—
The Journey of Death it is known as
in Mexico. This obsession with death is
evident even in the fiestas of the people.
Morbid skulls and skeletons made of
confectionery and candy are much in
demand on 2 November, the Day of
the Dead, when candlelight meals are
eaten on the graves of departed ones.
Pagan rituals of the Mayas and Incas, a
civilization steeped in blood sacrifice, had
lingered on to become intertwined with the
chains and torments of Christianity. Three
centuries under the lash of the Conquerors,
with little relief since Independence, had
bred in the peon not so much a fear as a
stoic reverence for death.

Black Pete lay on the mountainside
under the stars and pondered on the
tricks of fate that had brought him to
this unhappy country. He had known
much death himself. Every bullet had
its billet, as the saying goes. His was
overdue. He had diced with death for too
long. It would be untrue to say he could

face the forthcoming day with equanimity. Any man with the prospect before him in an hour or so of being torn apart by bullets in a very painful manner could hardly be particularly calm within. But a seething anger had overcome his fear. He had been a fool to allow Louisa to persuade him to be wed. No good could come of it. What future could they have together? No fool, as another maxim went, like an old fool. The intensity of her love, the beauty of the girl, had been impossible to resist. She was his bride. He did not like to think what they might be doing to her. It might have been better if he had not interfered, if she had been given to old Don Ignatio.

Before the sliver of moon began its fall he tightened the cinch of Jesus's saddle, fondly squeezed his ear, and eased himself up into the saddle. Brother Francisco watched silently at the cavern mouth, crossed himself and muttered a prayer as he rode off across the silvery plateau.

An echo of martial music seemed to ring in Black Pete's ears, echoes of cavalry charges in the war, the blare of trumpets at the bullring as the bull spurts out on to the newly-raked sand and the peons applaud with rapture—another example of the Spanish obsession with death—no, he did not feel like the matador, strutting in his finery, he had more akin with the bull, for whom, as he entered the arena, there was only one outcome: death. There would be more than sixty *rurales* and Wild Dogs down there waiting to do their work.

Straight-backed, determined, Pete went loping on down through the chasms...

A blood-red sun flickered over the horizon as Colonel Ferdinand Veraco breakfasted on fresh figs and black coffee. He had had his table and chair brought out to the edge of the village. He lit a cigarette and looked out across the field of skulls, out across the purple plain towards the dark and forbidding mountains, waiting for any sign of the horsemen...

'Bring the girl out,' he said.

The stone lid of the cellar was removed and Lousia was hauled out. Her teeth were chattering, her dark eyes distraught. She had spent the night huddled in a corner of the dank cellar in the pitch blackness, fighting off the scurrying rats. Her arms and body bore evidence of their bites.

The Wild Dogs gathered around and watched her. In the eyes of some was a sympathy, a *caballero's* regard for a beautiful girl. But the eyes of most of the former *bandidos* and ruffians were as cold and curious as a reptile's. They flickered with amused excitement when they heard the *jefe's* command.

'Strip her. Strip her naked.'

Louisa could not scream. Such was her dismay she could only gasp as the men tore her clothes roughly from her body, every stitch. To a girl brought up in a society of strict Roman Catholic modesty this was no small thing, to stand naked before these men's probing eyes.

'Ach!' one croaked. 'Look at those breasts.'

Louisa met their eyes dully, shivering as she tried to cover herself with her arms. Even so, there was a pride in her body's stance, the tilt of her head. Even if, within,

180

there was a dread of what they were about to do. The horror of the night would be preferable to the horror of that. Which one would take her first? She tried to murmur a silent prayer, to remind herself it was the spirit that counted, not the flesh. But it was hard.

'Tie her to the white horse.'

'What?' The *vicioso* with a face like a wolf, who had been drooling and grinning at her, appeared puzzled. 'What for, *jefe?*'

'Do as I say,' Colonel Veraco was immaculate in his best uniform. He wished to look good for the occasion. He smiled, icily, at Louisa. 'Well, my dear, have you changed your mind?'

She tossed her luxuriant curls. 'Never!' And stood shivering in the morning cold as the Wild Dogs gave howls of excitement, producing lariats, wanting to be the first to put their hands on her naked flesh. They crowded around her, fingers poking and feeling at her intimate parts as she struggled and was hauled up on to the back of Excellency, who stamped and snorted at the strange goings-on.

'Not that way,' Veraco shouted. 'Lay her on her back. Stretch her arms and legs back around him.'

As they did so, even he, the cold Veraco, who believed himself to be above such common lusts, could not subdue a lick of desire within him as Louisa was spreadeagled on the stallion's broad back and her beauty revealed to all.

'Right!' Veraco tried to make himself heard above the shouts and whistles, the deep-throated foulness of his men. 'Keep a firm hold on the bridle. Twenty of you men will take her out on to the plain. When you see the *gringo* coming you will display her to him. Don't wait to do battle. Gallop back with her to here. We will be waiting for you.'

The sun's rays were flickering violently into their eyes as twenty of the Wild Dogs vied for the privilege of being the ones who would ride out so they could feast their eyes longer on her, the pale sinuous-bodied young woman strapped across the white horse, her head thrown back, her dark curls tangled in his mane.

'The rest of you'—Veraco grinned as he watched the girl on the stallion go jogging out amid the wild whooping *vaqueros*—'take up positions in the buildings around the square. Give him no mercy. Shoot to kill.'

He beckoned for a glass of tequila. The trap had been set. What an ingenious bait! How could the *Americano* resist?

TWENTY

The cadaverous jaws of the wolf-faced Wild Dog drooled along Louisa's body as he leaned from his saddle to lick at her. 'Aiyee!' he screamed. 'You know what I do to you when this is over?' The rawhide bit into her body. She tried to turn her head away but he proceeded to splurge his cess-pool of evil thoughts upon her.

Suddenly a silence came over the other *vaqueros* as they looked across the plain and saw a spiral of dust approaching. It was like a cold wind coming down from the mountains. A dark figure of vengeance silhouetted against the fire of sunrise. The lurid filth from the mouth of the wolf-faced one ceased and he looked around to see what was happening. Excellency sensed something—perhaps the approach of

184

another stallion—and pranced nervously.

'It's him!' A fat-gutted, egg-bald *hombre* pulled his revolver as he watched the rider coming steadily on. 'We had better get going.'

'Pah! We are not frightened of one *gringo*. Let's show her to him.' The wolf-face snatched at the white horse's bridle, spurred his mustang, and went dancing the stallion back and forth, making him paw the air, displaying the painfully-bound girl. He cupped his hand and screamed at the man appearing from his shimmering sun haze, 'We got your girl, *gringo*. Take a good look. It will be your last.'

The other Wild Dogs began screaming insults as the dark rider drew closer. He was less than a quarter of a mile away when they saw through the daze that he had a rifle raised at his shoulder. A shot cracked out. There was the snarling whine of a bullet as the bald one was catapulted from his saddle. He lay kicking in the dust clutching at the bullet in his gut.

'Vamones!' the wolf-faced one shrieked. He jerked at the white stallion, who wanted

185

to go fight the black horse. 'Ride! Get outa here.'

The Wild Dogs charged away in a cloud of dust. Excellency was fiercely fighting the rope, the girl on his back jogged back and forth. Black Pete was close enough to see her pale nakedness. He bit his lip, squinted one eye along the sights as he rode, and squeezed out a .44 slug. The bullet ripped the man's sombrero off. The movement of his horse had made Pete misjudge.

'Damn them,' he whispered as the Wild Dog galloped after his *compagneros,* dragging the kicking Excellency and the spreadeagled girl behind him.

Two inches lower and they might have both escaped. Black Pete's knees gripped the stallion as he loped steadily on. He put the reins in his teeth, jerked down the Winchester's pump and, in rapid succession fired five more shots. He had the satisfaction of seeing two more men pitch from their saddles. He kicked his heels and put Jesus to a gallop, charging straight as an arrow after the retreating gunmen. He knew they were leading him into a trap but there was nothing he could do about it. And a white-hot fury had gripped him to see the way they were treating Louisa. At least she was still alive—but what life was it at the hands of these creatures?

Jesus had his neck outstretched, his mane flying, the steady rhythm of his hooves pounding the prairie. He was gaining on the *vaqueros*. His rider pumped his rifle and, as they looked back and hastily fired their revolvers, sent three more ruffians spinning into Eternity.

The *jefe* watched through his field-glasses as the crowd of snorting, prancing horsemen dashed towards Honi village. 'The fools!' he said. They had let their pursuer get too close. He licked his lips, nervously, and, as he did so, a bullet sent a man standing by his side spinning backwards, clutching at his eyes.

'Where in hell did that come from?' Another Wild Dog spun around beneath his big sombrero looking towards a small outcrop of rock a mile away! 'There's a sniper up there, *jefe.*'

A slug whistled through the air and cut off any more words the man might have had, cutting through his jugular and leaving him spouting blood into the sand.

'Get back!' Colonel Veraco shouted, running away towards the houses. 'Prepare to fire at will.' As an afterthought, fearing Ramón Corral's vengeance, he added, 'For God's sake don't shoot the girl!'

In the outcrop of rocks Nathan Strong peered through the long telescope of his M1857 Colt rifle and aimed at the *jefe* in his cream uniform who was hurrying back towards the ruined village. As he did so the *jefe* tripped on a skull in the soil and the slug went wide.

'Shee-it!' Nathan drawled. The six in his magazine were spent. He put the rifle in its boot and jumped on to his old cowhorse. 'Get 'em, boy,' he cried, and went charging down from the rocks, closing in in a V-line to intercept the galloping men. He began blamming away alongside of them with his old Navy Colt and three more tumbled to be stomped to pieces by churning hooves.

The Wild Dogs had pulled a wagon

over to block one end of the street, and several knelt waiting for the oncoming horde. Across the plain from behind them Melody and Miguel charged, Cajeme and Yaqui horsemen hard on their heels. The *vaqueros* behind the wagon turned to meet them but it was too late, they were cut down like dogs.

All was a mêlée of confusion, rolling gunsmoke, clouds of dust, screaming horses, the crashing of revolvers as the Wild Dogs poured into the village square, leapt from their mustangs, and tried to find cover. They were unprepared for the presence of Miguel and the Yaquis. Nor did Melody's six-shooter often miss its mark.

Into it all sped the magnificent white stallion, the naked girl trussed to his back, the wolf-face man hanging on to them. He leapt his mustang away down an alleyway, and scrambled the horses out of the village to seek escape back towards Fortune del Rey and more friendly territory.

Colonel Veraco took in what was happening and silently cursed. Panic filled him as he saw the *gringo* on the black stallion erupt into the square, a Smith and Wesson in each hand, shooting straight-armed, blasting the men in the ruins out of life, into death. He was like a dark whirlwind of vengeance. Invincible.

The colonel steadied his revolver, or tried to, for his hand was shaking. The bullet whined past the head of the *renegado*, who turned to see where it had come from. Veraco panicked, backing away through the burned house, tripping, scrambling, gaining his chestnut, hurriedly climbing on to the mare, kicking in his spurs and heading after the wolf-faced *vaquero* and the girl strapped to the white stallion. Racing away, seeking only his own safety.

Where had the white stallion gone? Black Pete vacated the wild turmoil of battling men, bounded Jesus out of the village, high-stepped him over a ploughed field of skulls, through brakes of bamboo, and set off in pursuit of the dust cloud, streaking away across the plain. Both his revolvers were emptied. He had had no time to reload. He thrust them back in his holsters and slapped Jesus into a gallop, hanging low over his neck as the wind tore at his clothing.

There was no way he could catch them on the flat. But, if he took to the high ground? He urged Jesus up a rocky slope and picked his way across a *mesa* in the hope of intercepting them. He hauled Jesus in on a cliff edge, pulled out his Winchester. The magazine was empty. He took a bullet from his belt, inserted it into the breech. One was all he needed. Carefully, he took a bead, and fired. He gave a gasp of relief to see the Wild Dog collapse over his mustang's neck, and the white stallion go careering on free.

As she knew herself cast free, and she glimpsed the tall horseman on the clifftop, in spite of the pain in her torn arms and legs, a sensation of ecstasy filled Louisa's body. She felt the muscles of the stallion churning away beneath her, heard the reverberation of his hooves, smelt his sweat, sensed his mane flying in her eyes, her naked body responding to his as the stallion surged away across the purple sage.

Pete thrust the Winchester back in its boot. Veraco had heard the shot and had turned the chestnut's head, tacking away from them. Pete ploughed Jesus, on his haunches, down the almost vertical cliff, skiing into a pile of scree at the foot, and set off after the *jefe politico*.

The chestnut was fast, but not as nimble or as strong as Jesus on this mountain terrain. And, perhaps the fine mare's haunches gave the stallion an added impetus to catch her? Whatever, Pete was certainly the more skilled rider. Gradually, as they entered a narrow *cañon* he gained on Veraco. Swirling his lariat, he sent it spinning over the colonel's shoulders, hefted him thudding from the saddle. He leaped from Jesus's back and let him go chasing after the chestnut.

'It's just you and me, Veraco.' He gritted the words out as he jerked the winded colonel to his knees. 'It's all over. But you ain't gonna go easy.'

Ferdinand Veraco looked up at the long-legged cowboy towering over him. He was uncoiling a bullwhip that he had hanging over his shoulder. A lead-tipped bullwhip. 'No, please'—he choked on the words—'I will make you rich. I will give you anything.'

'I don't need anything. Anything you got. You've offered your last *mordida*.' Pete snaked the whip out, cracking it in the air, making the *jefe* raise his hands, silently begging for mercy. 'You're gonna go the way Louisa's father went.'

Veraco's arms were pinned to his side by the lariat. But even if he could have reached for his revolver he would have been too terrified to try. Was it the first lick of the whip that was the most excruciating? It snaked out around his throat, cutting in to the flesh. The second teased the scarlet epaulette from his uniform. The third tore through the cream jacket, ripping into the flesh.

'No!' Veraco screamed.

He toppled backwards, tried to wriggle away, escape the sting of fire.

'Exquisite, ain't it? Ain't that what you called it? How about that?' The dark-bearded cowboy's face was gritted tense as the lash cut into the crawling man's body and blood seeped into the fine uniform. Again and again the rawhide cracked. It was as if he could feel the burning pain himself, could see his wife burning as the rafters of their home toppled down upon her, as the vigilantes charged about him in the darkness, as the noose seared about his neck, choking him. Before him he could see the faces of the peons swinging on ropes from the branches, the splattered brains and skulls as the *rurales* charged across the ploughed field, the wild shouts of the butchers, the smile of the *jefe* as he sipped his tequila. 'What's the matter, Veraco? You're not smiling now.'

He grunted for breath and stood poised as the bloody *jefe* rolled over and groaned, his legs twitching, his mouth gaping like a stranded fish. 'Let's see the white of your bone, Veraco. Isn't that the way to do it? Isn't that the exquisite way! How many lashes it gonna take afore you die? Another thirty?'

He cracked the whip and was about to lay into the trembling man again when a

194

shot rang out behind him, almost nicking his ear. Blood coughed from Veraco's thin lips as the slug ploughed into his chest. His eyes glimmered on the dark cowboy for seconds as if wondering who he was, where he had come from. And he slumped back, the eyes going opaque. The *jefe* was dead.

'It's over, Pete.'

Nathan sat his horse and jammed his smoking Navy Colt back into its holster. He stepped down in his batwing *chaparejos* and poked his foot at the lacerated man. 'The buzzards can have him.'

Pete looked into the piercing blue eyes and, whispered, 'Yeah, I guess so.' He tossed the whip down on to the bloody corpse. He heard the whicker of another horse and looked behind him. Louisa was straddling the back of the white stallion. Her ropes had been cut away and she sat bareback. An old saddle blanket covered her nakedness and her hair tumbled down about her shoulders. Her sloe-black eyes surveyed the scene, sadly. But there was a glimmer of hope in them as they met his.

'I guess that's got all of my hatred outa me. And, at least, your father's spirit can rest at peace.'

'I guess so, Pete,' she whispered.

'C'mon.' He jumped up behind her on to the white horse, hugged an arm around her waist and took the bridle-reins. 'Let's go look for Jesus.'

They followed the tracks of the stallion and chestnut and soon heard a whinnying and snorting, and Excellency began joining in, stamping and biting, as they saw Jesus busily mounting the mare, his teeth gnawing at her neck in a kind of bliss as he did so.

'Whoa, boy,' Pete crooned to Excellency, holding him back. 'Your turn will come one of these days.'

They all laughed as they waited for the horses to finish, lassoed them, and headed back to Honi. There they found Nathan and Miguel, Cajeme and the Yaquis victorious. Those Wild Dogs who hadn't been killed had scattered far and wide.

Black Pete saw a notice tacked to a post. *Reward—4,000 pesos—Los Quatros*

Renegados Americanos. He ripped it away, tucked it into his macinaw. 'Guess I'll keep this as a souvenir. Time we were on our way.'

TWENTY-ONE

When they had rested and feasted, when Louisa's cuts, burns and rat bites had been tended, and she was soothed by Pete, and dressed in a dead *vaquero's* clothes, they rode out with the Yaqui back to their mountain stronghold. They bid *adios* and good luck to Cajeme, and waved 'so long' to Brother Francisco. He watched them head up into the Sierra Madre and shouted, '*Vaya con Dios,* my children.'

Cajeme sat astride Excellency—Black Pete had insisted he have him on account of Excellency and Jesus just not getting on—and his solemn face, broke, for once, into a smile. 'They were good fighters,' he said.

Brother Francisco took his mule and made

his way back down to the towns and villages of Sonora. Over the next months he stood on street corners and spoke out for the rights of the peons and Indians.

Inevitably, one day a bunch of *rurales* surrounded him. 'Here is the priest who has been preaching treason,' one screamed.

The new *jefe politico* looked down at the grizzle-haired man in his hair smock, standing there barefoot, his little dog barking furiously at them. 'Put him up against that wall and shoot him,' he said.

'It's no good, my friend'—Brother Francisco bent down and soothed the terrier—'they don't understand what we say.'

He crossed himself as he stood against the wall, the little dog squatted at his side. Six of the *rurales* formed a firing squad. 'Viva Mexico!' Francisco shouted. The shots rang out and the priest crumpled back against the wall, his arms outstretched, his robe bloodied.

When the *rurales* had gone he lay there. None of the peons dared move him. As night came on the little terrier nestled beside him, rested his head on his chest, his eyes anxious. He gave a whimper of sorrow. He did not know what to do, where to go. Eventually, no doubt, he would become one of the pariah curs who roamed the garbage dumps.

When they had crossed the mountains Pete and Louisa, Nathan and Melody, and Miguel, decided to head further south into Old Mexico, through Chivata to Sacramento, following the course of the Rio Conchos into Chihuahua, skirting the seven million acre estate of the State governor. On they wandered as the weeks passed, on through Torreon, Saltillo and Conception del Cro until they crossed the line into San Luis Potosi.

Here the valleys between the high hills were richly tropical, parrots squabbled in the trees, and six-inch butterflies in exquisite colours fluttered through the groves. They reached the village of San Juan. There was a terrible commotion going on in the streets, bugles blaring, drums being banged. The whole population appeared to be drunk, grinning and dancing, shuffling back and forth, men in long ponchos and straw hats whirling their scabby mules around, making even the poor animals dance. Even the children seemed to be intoxicated. Firecrackers were tossed under their horses' hooves as they rode into the narrow streets and screams of excitement, the strumming of guitars, thrummed from the *cantinas*.

'Hey, *señor*, what's the celebration?' Pete called.

'Nothing, *amigo*. We are having fiesta. Today we are happy. Tomorrow, who knows?' the man replied, offering a jug to them.

'Hey!' Nathan took a pull, and wiped his mouth. 'Maybe this is where we start mining for silver.'

'Maybe,' Pete grinned.

'Meester'—a little boy pulled at Miguel's trousers '—you wan' my seester? Only seven pesos.'

'Yai-yai-yay!' Miguel whooped and

jumped from his horse. 'This is our sort of place. This is more like Me-hico! Lead on, *muchacho.*'

'I sure am tired of ridin',' Pete scowled, stepping down and sprawling out at a chair and table on the sidewalk. 'I'm gonna rest my carcase here awhile.'

He lit a cheroot and squinted through the smoke at them, as Louisa, Melody and Nathan joined him. 'This looks like a real friendly town. Don't reckon we'll have any trouble here awhile.'

'Don't say that, you ole buzzard,' Nathan said. 'You know trouble jest comes lookin' fer you.'

'Not this time.' Pete eyed the mescal-crazed population in their colourful costumes. 'This time me and Louisa here's on a kinda delayed honeymoon.'

The little fat *patron* came bustling out to them. 'Bring food and wine, the best you got in the house,' Pete said. 'And, *señor,* you wouldn't know somewhere there's a nice big feather bed, wouldja?'

'What you gonna do there?' Nathan chuckled.

'We're gonna enjoy ourselves while you go look for a silver mine,' Pete drawled. 'And if any *jefe politico* pokes in his nose—shoot him on sight!'

AFTERWORD

President Porfirio Diaz ruled with an iron fist for another thirty years. He was lauded by the heads of governments. Theodore Roosevelt, the cowboy president, claimed there was 'no greater contemporary statesman'. Ramón Corral, governor of Sonora, became for his services, Vice-President of Mexico. The massacres and injustices described in this novel are based on historical events, although the time-scale has been telescoped. The programme of genocide against the Yaqui went on. It was reckoned if they lasted a year in irons on the Yucatan plantations they made good workers. Cajeme was captured in 1887 and shot 'attempting to escape'. Many more were killed. Mexican strikers who dared to ask for a wage increase were shot down in the streets. In the early years of the twentieth century Pancho Villa and

Emiliano Zapata defied the regime. The people rose up like a hurricane to support the revolution and Diaz was swept from power. The struggles continued for many years, Villa and Zapata both meeting violent deaths...such was Mexico.

The publishers hope that this book has given you enjoyable reading. Large Print Books are especially designed to be as easy to see and hold as possible. If you wish a complete list of our books, please ask at your local library or write directly to: Dales Large Print Books, Long Preston, North Yorkshire, BD23 4ND, England.

This Large Print Book for the Partially sighted, who cannot read normal print, is published under the auspices of

THE ULVERSCROFT FOUNDATION